Is Stacie making the right decision?

Out of the corner of her eye, Stacie could see Brad shift his position so he could look at her when he spoke, "I love you, too, Stacie. You know I do. But I just don't see how I can pick up and move to Thomasville and start all over again. I've worked so hard to get a business going here."

"So what do we do now?" Stacie could hardly hold back the tears; she knew what his answer would be.

"We can't get married and live 200 miles apart. If I'm going to provide for us, I have to live here." Even though he held his voice steady with conviction, Stacie could hear the sadness in Brad's words.

SUSANNAH HAYDEN is the pen name of a versatile and gifted author of fiction and biography for both adults and children. Her recent inspirational romances include the popular *Summer's Wind Blowing* and *Spring Waters Rushing*.

Books by Susannah Hayden

ROMANCE READER—TWO BOOKS IN ONE

RR9—Summer's Wind Blowing & Spring Waters Rushing

A Matter of Choice

Susannah Hayden

Heartsong Presents

ISBN 1-55748-356-6

one

The alarm clock buzzed loudly for the second time on that gray, drizzly, early March morning. Stacie Hanaken groaned, rolled over, and stretched her slender arm to hush the abrasive intrusion on her sound slumber. Her limbs heavy with sleep, it seemed an extraordinary effort to reach as far as her bedside table to find the right button.

When the irritating buzz finally stopped, she pulled her head out from under the pillow and squinted with one blue eye at the large red numbers of her digital alarm clock—and then sat bolt upright. Could it possibly be that late? Stacie rubbed her eyes with the heels of her hands and looked again. There was no question she would be late for work if she wasted even one more minute. Quickly she threw off the covers and scurried toward the bathroom.

On her way to the shower she grabbed bunches of her thick, coppery hair and twisted them into a haphazard knot on the top of her head. Her hair, the color of a shiny new penny, was the first feature most people commented on. It hung smooth and silky to the middle of her back with a controlled wavy fullness which no hairdresser had ever been able to duplicate for her envious friends. Nevertheless, Stacie occasionally thought of cutting it short into a style which would look more mature. After all, she was not a college girl anymore; she was a career woman who had just accepted an exciting promotion.

Brad had always liked her hair long; she supposed that was why she never gave in to the urge to cut it. She enjoyed having long hair but lately had come to think of it as more trouble than it was worth. Like today; it needed to be washed, but she did not have the time. Stacie stopped for a moment at the shower door and put the final pin in place. As she checked to be sure her hair was securely off her neck, she could almost see Brad's face next to her own in the mirror. She still could not believe that he had actually broken their engagement!

They met when Stacie was in her third year of college and Brad was a carpenter working for a contractor who was building a new dormitory on the campus. It was love at first sight, and everyone agreed that if two people ever belonged together, it was Brad and Stacie. To support herself, she worked nearly full-time in the college personnel office while she also carried a full load of course work. She typed papers for other students, babysat the children of her professors— whatever she could do to be able to stay in school and graduate with her class. She turned down promising dates over and over again for the sake of her school work and her dream of becoming a social worker.

On that crisp fall day with red and gold leaves swirling in the breeze and crunching underfoot, Stacie rushed to the administration building to deliver a completed project. Impulsively, she took a shortcut through the construction area and literally stumbled over Brad's shiny red tool box, nearly sending 200 sheets of neatly-typed pages flying all over the campus. Brad caught her elbow just in time to steady her, and when she looked into those dark eyes, darker than any she had ever seen, she knew she had just met—or was about to meet—an exceptional man. His matching dark brown hair curled softly at his temples and brushed the top of his collar in the back. He smiled in an amused way at the pretty coed he had just caught hold of; she felt a firm strength in his arms and an immediate comfort in his presence.

Brad invited her to dinner that night, and again for the next night. Stacie accepted, forgetting all about using her school work as a reason not to date. Although he had not finished college himself, Brad admired Stacie's motivation and determination to earn a college degree. In spite of the fact that it was an uphill battle for her and that most of her classmates had easier circumstances. Then, when she landed a job in the public service office of the small town of St. Mary's where they lived, he beamed with pride and threw a party to celebrate. On the eve of her graduation and the beginning of her career, he tenderly asked her to be his wife and, without a moment's hesitation, she joyfully accepted. For a long time, she had been hoping he would propose, but when the actual moment came, she still found it hard to believe that someone as wonderful as Bradley Bauman Davis truly wanted to spend his life with her.

Stacie shook herself out of her reverie and turned on the water. She stepped into the steamy shower stall and turned the water up as hot and hard as she could stand it hoping that both the heat and pressure would get rid of her nervous tension. Often, as now, she would sing or pray aloud as she stood in the shower, soothing body and spirit at one time.

Today, however, it was not working. All she could think about was Brad and how much she had missed him in these last two months. He was a man of contagious ambition and surging leadership, two qualities about him which she had soon come to love. He was quick to assess a difficult situation and make practical suggestions which invariably led to solving the problem. Somehow it always seemed natural for other people to follow his directions and it seemed natural for him to step in where leadership was lacking. Between the two of them, Stacie and Brad had the energy, initiative, and determination for any task which might come up. They both looked forward to spending many years together as a loving, united team.

It was with happy anticipation that Stacie had phoned Brad one day two months ago to suggest they have a celebration dinner. When he asked what they would be celebrating, she smiled to herself and told him he would just have to wait to find out. She would not satisfy his curiosity until they were face to face over a table at O'Reilly's, eating identical corned beef sandwiches.

Stacie arrived at the restaurant and saw Brad's second-hand truck, with its once-bright red color sadly faded, parked near the door. Grimy as it was, she could not resist dragging her fingers lightly across the hood. She loved to be near something that belonged to Brad almost as much as she loved to be with Brad himself. Her mouth turned up in pleasure, she pushed open the door and glanced around the cozy dining room. When she found him sitting at the table with a puzzled look on his face, she unashamedly kissed him and tousled his curly hair.

"What was that for?" Brad asked, pleased but still curious.

"That, sweetheart, was a celebration kiss." Stacie took off the light gray jacket she was wearing and hung it over the back of her chair before sitting down. She reached for Brad's hands. "I have some terrific news!"

Brad was clearly intrigued and amused by her enthusiasm. "Well, I guess you'd better clue me in, so both of us can go around grinning like Cheshire cats."

"Do you remember meeting my boss, Jack Rogers, at the company party?" Brad nodded, and Stacie continued. "He came into my office today and offered me a promotion."

"That's wonderful, Stacie! You've been there only eight months. I know you do a great job, and I don't know anyone else as dedicated as you are, but a promotion . . . that's great news!" He leaned across the table, kissed her, and then, as he often did to her, he affectionately thumped her nose with his index finger. "Tell me more. What's the new job?"

"You know I've been working on that research project on homeless people in the state . . . studying causes and possible solutions. Now I'm going to get to do something besides just paperwork!" Her eyes were bright with excitement. "They want me to be the assistant director of a new shelter for the homeless. It's not supposed to open for about six months so I'll have some time for training first."

Brad leaned back in his chair and looked at her proudly. "You'll be perfect for the job . . . you're so organized and you really care about what you're doing." He stopped and tilted his head in a questioning way. "Isn't there a homeless shelter already here in St. Mary's? This is not a very big town. Are there really enough homeless people to need a second one?"

"That's the rest of the news," Stacie said. "The job is not here in St. Mary's. The new shelter will be in Thomasville."

Stacie was too excited to admit to herself that Brad tensed up at the mention of Thomasville. Eager to give him more of the details, she kept talking. "The agency has been wanting to do this for a long time. Thomasville is a good spot for a new shelter because there aren't any within miles of there. I'm still in shock that they asked me—"

Brad cut her off abruptly. "But Stacie," he said with his

voice low and the proud smile gone from his face, "that's nearly 200 miles from here."

She hardly knew what to say. When she spoke, her voice was barely audible. "Yes, I know where Thomasville is. I've lived in this state all my life." Stacie looked down at her lap and twisted the corner of her napkin between her fingers until it was shredded. It was obvious to her now that Brad was not reacting the way she had hoped . . . and expected.

After an excruciating and long silence, during which they hardly moved a muscle, Brad said, "Well, it's very flattering that they thought of you for this position. It's too bad you can't accept."

Stacie jerked her head up and, with her mouth open in disbelief, stared at Brad. "I haven't given them an answer yet. Of course I wanted to talk with you. But it's the kind of job I've been preparing for and praying for . . . I can't just dismiss it without serious thought."

When the waiter came and said his familiar hello, Brad and Stacie ordered the corned beef sandwiches and sauerkraut that they usually relished. But neither of them ate much—or said much—and the evening ended early.

Remembering that she had overslept, Stacie abruptly shut off the shower and stepped out of the stall. As she wrapped her flannel robe around her, she wished she had thought to start the coffee before getting in the shower; now there would be no time. When the pins were out of her hair and it cascaded gracefully, she started brushing it and thinking about what she should wear to work. Was her pink blouse clean? It would go well with her new linen navy suit and the navy pumps which were so much more comfortable than those brown shoes that hurt her feet.

The drizzle had turned to a steady rain, and Stacie grimaced at the thought that she would need her khaki raincoat and umbrella. She moved to the closet and methodically removed the clothes she would wear that day. Once dressed, she added small gold earrings and a simple gold chain. Although she still did not feel enthusiastic about leaving the apartment, a glance in the mirror told her that she appeared ready. She blew out a sigh and straightened her slouched shoulders, determined that people would not know the depth of her pain simply by looking at her. A guarded, private person, Stacie had not talked very much about her engagement to the people she worked with. Some of them had noticed her suddenly bare ring finger, but few realized the connection between her promotion and the broken engagement.

Accepting Brad's marriage proposal was the easiest decision Stacie had ever made but agreeing to take the new job was the most difficult decision of her life. Stacie was convinced that God wanted her to work at the new shelter in Thomasville but she could understand Brad's reluctance for her to accept it. He had his own contractor's business now, and the St Mary's area was bursting with potential new growth. There would be plenty of work there and he would make a very comfortable income for them to live on. He insisted that if they got married he would provide for them, and it made sense for him to do that in St. Mary's.

The night Stacie told Brad she had decided to accept the promotion there was a twisted knot in her stomach. Unspoken tension hung in the air, and she had been dreading this moment more and more as it got closer. But she knew she had to do it. She picked up their dishes from the small table in her apartment and carried them to the sink. Slowly she walked back into the living room where Brad was waiting for her.

"This is very hard for me, Brad," she started, not even able to look him in the eye. "I love you with all my heart, and I really thought the Lord had brought us together. We've had two incredible years, and I can't live my life without you. But I also think the Lord wants me to take this job. It's such a strong feeling—I can't explain it completely, but I know I can't just ignore it."

Out of the corner of her eye, Stacie could see Brad shift his position so he could look at her when he spoke. "I love you, too, Stacie. You know I do. But I just don't see how I can pick up and move to Thomasville and start all over again. I've worked so hard to get a business going here."

"So what do we do now?" Stacie could hardly hold back the tears; she knew what his answer would be.

"We can't get married and live 200 miles apart. If I'm going to provide for us, I have to live here." Even though he held his voice steady with conviction, Stacie could hear the sadness in Brad's words.

They sat together on the couch in Stacie's apartment—the country-blue and gray-plaid couch with the ruffle around the bottom that they had picked out together as their first piece of furniture. To her surprise, Brad reached for her and drew her close. All they could do was hold each other and share in their mutual pain. Clearly, Brad did not want her to move away, but just as clearly, she had to do it.

Devastated by the impasse they had reached, Stacie hoarsely asked, "Do you want your ring back?"

Brad gently lifted Stacie's left hand and wrapped his fingers around hers. "No, it's your ring. It no longer means that we're getting married, but it still means I love you, and I don't think I'll ever stop." He moved his hand to her chin and lifted her face, streaked with tears. Putting his lips softly on hers he kissed her long and slowly and then picked up his jacket and left without speaking again.

Now, Stacie stood staring at that same couch. They had bought it together just after having announced their engagement. It was supposed to have symbolized the beginning of their life together, and they had spent many evenings on it, resting in each other's arms as they talked of their future together. They had thought about other furniture, the fine home Brad would someday build for them, their work in the church, her work in the community. Brad supported Stacie's desire to continue working at St. Mary's public service office and he had always seemed to understand how important it was for her to be helping other people. Only on that painful night did she at last realize that his understanding had limitations.

Standing immobilized in her living room, Stacie put her fingers to her lips and could almost feel the tenderness of Brad's kiss and his work-calloused hand under her chin. How she loved him! *Would she really be able to move to Thomasville and start a new life without him?* Brad was the first and only man she had ever loved, and it was incomprehensible that she should ever care for anyone else with the same passionate intensity. She really believed she was following the Lord's will by taking this new job. *Did this mean she would always be alone, always longing for the touch and companionship of the man she loved? Had she made a horrible mistake when she accepted the new job?*

The phone jangled loudly and Stacie jumped involuntarily. She glanced at her watch and thought that it was too early in the morning for someone to be calling, but she crossed the room and picked up the phone on the second ring.

"Stacie?"

"Oh, hi, Megan." Stacie was relieved to hear the voice of her best friend and relaxed into the tufted blue chair next to the window.

"I hadn't talked to you all week, so I wanted to see how you are. I hope it's not too early to call."

"You know you can call any time, Megan. But I'm fine, really. You don't have to keep checking up on me." Stacie instantly regretted the sarcasm in her own voice. She fingered the edge of the white eyelet curtain and looked with growing dread at the downpour outside the window.

Megan, in her characteristic way, ignored the edginess in Stacie's words. "Well, I happen to know you are not so fine as you say, but we don't have to talk about that now. I also wanted to know if you're planning to go to Bible study tonight."

"I suppose I should. I've missed the last two weeks. But it's so hard. . . ." Stacie knew Megan would understand how difficult it was for her to go to Bible study when she knew Brad would be there. Yet, the group included her closest friends and she did not want to drop out completely.

"I'll pick you up and we'll go together," Megan said, her voice deliberately cheerful.

"Thanks, Megan. I'm sorry I snapped at you. You're my best friend in the world, you know that."

"See you tonight, friend."

Megan hung up, but somehow just hearing her voice had made Stacie feel better. Sensible, solid, faithful Megan, her roommate from college and the dear friend who was supposed to have been her maid of honor in another few weeks. Stacie had been so pleased that Megan and Brad got along well and that neither of them had resented her intimate relationship with the other. She smiled as she remembered how they would often join in teasing her about some peculiar habit or when she said something that did not come out quite right. She had been blessed with these two people who cared deeply for her and had grown fond of each other as well.

Stacie now had only two minutes before she absolutely had to leave. She snapped on the radio, and as she gulped down a glass of orange juice, she heard the announcement that the rain was not expected to let up until sometime the next day.

"Ugh!" she said aloud and reluctantly got out the umbrella from the small closet next to the door of the apartment. She picked up her briefcase and purse and, making sure to lock the door behind her, hesitantly ventured out into the rain.

two

Somehow Stacie muddled through the day at work—and even managed a reasonable degree of productivity. Her tiny office, once part of a larger suite that had been subdivided, was packed with the evidence of her hard work. The bookshelves overflowed with college textbooks, government reports, census data, and papers by national experts that predicted sociological trends. Snapshots splattered the walls— pictures of her during her internship in Chicago and photos of the St. Mary's shelter and the people who stayed there, some of them for months at a time. On the corner of her desk was the stack of bulging case files that she was handling.

Stacie felt that if she could not find satisfaction in her work, then there really would be no point to sacrificing her relationship with Brad. So, at the office, she was meticulously attentive to the tasks before her. Easily she could have closed her office door and allowed herself to lapse into isolated self-pity—everyone would have thought that she was just hard at work preparing for her transfer to Thomasville. But, instead, she propped the door open first thing in the morning and made sure she kept herself busy. While working, she could hear the rapid clicks of computer keyboards, the hum of the photocopier, the bleeps of the new telephone system. Periodically, she would smell the inviting aroma from the coffeepot in the back room and would go out and refill her large mug.

The reports spread across her desk were overwhelming. Accurate records on homeless people were difficult to keep, but the studies showed a definite increase in the number of women and children who suddenly were without a place to call home. Since the new shelter in Thomasville would be a haven specifically for women and children, Stacie had buried herself with information about other programs which were effective in helping these one-parent families find jobs and establish new homes. She continued to handle some of the routine work of the shelter in St. Mary's, but most of her time was now devoted to preparing for the move to Thomasville. The building would be ready when she arrived, but it would be up to the new staff to devise a program to attack the problem.

Lunchtime came. Stacie made sure to save the notes she was collecting on her computer and pushed her chair back from the desk. On Tuesdays and Thursdays she spent her lunch hour working as a volunteer in the food line that was offered by her agency. A look out the window told her she would still need her umbrella, so, disgruntled, she took it off its hook and left the office.

Around the corner at the shelter, the lunch crowd was already gathering. Stacie pushed open the door and was nearly run over by a four-year-old boy, exuberantly charging at her.

"Joey!" she said, laughing. "Slow down." She stooped to give Joey a quick hug. "How's my favorite boy?"

"I'm hungry!" Joey reached around Stacie's neck with both arms and squeezed.

"Then you came to the right place." She stood up and took hold of his hand. "Let's go see what's for lunch."

Stacie got Joey settled with his mother and his baby sister and then took her place behind the serving table. Mounds of tangled spaghetti noodles filled several serving platters and steam rose from the pots of sauce nearby. The line of hungry people moved steadily. Stacie was always amazed at how many people came for this meal, even in a town as small as St. Mary's, and that many of them would not have another meal until the next day.

Joey and his family had been coming to the shelter for several weeks. The energetic little boy with blond hair and blue eyes chattered constantly and was a favorite of everyone who worked in the lunch line. As she served the meals, Stacie could not resist looking over at Joey every few minutes. He seemed to sense when she was looking and gave her a friendly wave every time, sometimes loudly calling out "Hi, Stacie!" before his mother hushed him. His blue pants were too short and the knees were looking worn; the thin gray sweater he wore was too big. Stacie often thought how easy it would be to feel overwhelmed by the impossible task of solving the problems of all the people like Joey's family. But she was not discouraged. Helping even one family, or even one little boy, was a start. She knew there were many more little boys like Joey in Thomasville.

When she got home from work, Stacie was exhausted. The rainy weather had put her in the mood for a bowl of hot soup for supper, a favorite and frequent meal choice in the evenings. She took a container of homemade beefy vegetable soup from the freezer and emptied it into a pan on the stove. As she stood and stirred it, waiting for it to thaw, she worked at changing mental gears from the demands of the office and the emotions of the shelter to the challenge of attending a Bible study where she would see Brad. It would not be the first time they had seen each other since her decision to move away, but she was not sure it would be any easier than the other times.

As she sat and ate, alone, she worked hard not to think of all the suppers she and Brad had shared at that little table. Homemade beefy vegetable soup was actually his favorite, and for a long time after their break-up she had not been able to bring herself to eat any of the supply in her freezer.

Stacie considered calling Megan and saying she could not go, but resisted the urge. Instead, she changed into comfortable jeans and a bright blue sweatshirt and sat in the chair by the window to listen for Megan's familiar toot of the horn. Her friend was prompt, as Stacie had expected she would be.

"You sure you're up to this?" Megan asked as she pulled away from the curb.

"I have to be," Stacie replied. "I can't give up my whole life just because of what happened with Brad. I'll be lonely enough when I move away; I don't want to feel that way now." She looked at her friend—an easy-going kindergarten teacher with her brown hair tied in a casual ponytail and baggy clothes hiding her athletic build—and was stabbed by the realization of how much she would miss Megan. Thrown together as roommates by the routine workings of college administration, Megan and Stacie had cemented their relationship by suffering together through term papers, bad dates, final exams, and career choices. They both had been ecstatic to find jobs in St. Mary's where they could be near one another. In a few months though, Stacie would be leaving behind more than Brad when she moved to Thomasville. And, without Brad, she would feel Megan's absence even more acutely.

"I think it's Brad's turn to lead the discussion tonight," Megan said softly, "so I'm sure he'll be there."

Stacie turned her head away and looked out the window;

trees and telephone poles whizzed by. True to the forecast, the drizzle had not let up all day, and the view was gray and shrouded in the early evening dusk. "There will be twenty other people there," she said. "I probably won't even have to talk to him. Just stay right with me, please."

"I won't leave your side." Both Megan's tone and words were very reassuring.

Brad's shiny new blue work van, a symbol of his business success with his young company's colorful logo emblazoned on both sides, was already parked in the church lot near the door. Brad had wanted to trade in his old pickup for a long time. Apparently, business was finally good enough that he had done it. On the one hand Stacie was glad for his success; on the other hand, the sleek new van was a visible and indisputable argument that his business was going well enough to make moving away seem foolish.

Megan purposefully pulled her small used and dented car into a space at the far end of the lot, and the two young women walked together into the church building. The lounge where the group of young adults met every Thursday evening was filling up, and the room buzzed with clusters of conversations about college courses and career challenges. Megan gave Stacie a characteristic cheerful smile and nudged her toward one of the groups.

They chatted amiably with several other people, but Stacie had to work hard to concentrate on the conversation. Someone asked her about her new job but, as she answered the question, she was not sure her thoughts were coming out coherently. Out of the corner of her eye she saw Brad sitting on a couch talking quietly with a couple of women from the college. She knew it was ridiculous and chastised herself immediately, but, involuntarily, jealousy welled up inside her. Although his dark head was bent in earnest, attentive conversation, she saw his eyes flicker briefly when she looked in his direction. Immediately, she turned away; still, his face floated before her, his familiar and attractive features replacing those of the young man who was talking to her.

She was startled for a moment when she heard Brad's voice urging everyone in the room to take their seats and get comfortable so the Bible study could begin. As always, the others accepted his leadership and lowered themselves into the menagerie of donated couches and chairs scattered around the room. Stacie and Megan sat together on a small, tattered, beige love seat, their Bibles poised in their laps, awaiting direction from Brad.

Brad read the passage and launched into a preliminary explanation of several verses before asking some questions for the group to discuss. While he spoke, Stacie could legitimately keep her eyes on the Bible in her lap, but, during the discussion, it was more difficult to keep from looking at Brad. Mechanically, she turned her head from side to side as people around the room joined in and tried to follow the flow of the discussion. She used to be one of the most vocal participants in these stimulating talks, but tonight she could barely make sense of the main points people were making. Periodically, Stacie sensed Megan glancing at her and forced herself to smile or nod so her friend would know she was all right. Stacie knew she had been right to come. Although the people in the group were stunned at their broken engagement, they respected and cared for Brad and her and did not want either of them to drop out of the group.

When the meeting was almost finished, Stacie noticed Pastor Banning slip into the room and sit in a chair near the door. After the closing prayer, Brad motioned for the pastor to come up and address the group. Pastor Banning walked around to the front of the room to explain his purpose.

"Several of you have told me you would like to take on a special project as a group," he said, "and I think I have just the thing for you to do. I met a woman last week who could really use your help."

He went on to explain that there was an old youth camp, the old Family Homestead, about twenty miles out of town owned by a woman named Margaret Barrows. For many years she and her husband ran the camp, but when he became ill, she closed it to take care of him. Recently, he passed away, and the elderly Mrs. Barrows wanted very much to see the camp restored and back in operation. She has enough money available for the restoration if she can find donated labor. There would be cleaning, landscaping, painting, and construction work to be done but, if the group would take on the project, perhaps the camp could be ready before summer.

Stacie was caught up in the enthusiasm pulsing through the group. If the goal was to refurbish the camp before summer, she could help before moving away for her new job. She did not mind strenuous physical labor—in fact, she enjoyed it. At the mention of construction work, attention had shifted noticeably to Brad. Everyone seemed to assume he would head up the work project and he seemed to have already accepted the assignment. Megan looked questioningly at Stacie.

"It's okay, Megan," Stacie whispered. "I want to do this. It sounds like there's a lot to be done; I want to help."

Someone started circulating sign-up sheets for various tasks, and Stacie and Megan both signed up to go out the next weekend to scrub the cabins and do odd jobs. Long after the meeting was officially over, the group's members stayed in the lounge planning work dates and making lists of the supplies they would need. Stacie was pulled out of her self-consciousness and listened carefully to the suggestions Brad was making. Without realizing the moment of the shift, she had begun to participate fully in the zealous planning.

Knowing that tomorrow was a work day, Stacie at last suggested to Megan that they should leave. Megan nodded her agreement and they gathered up their books and notes. They were almost to the door when someone called Megan's name.

"I'll be right there, Stace," Megan said, and turned her attention away.

Stacie leaned against the wall contentedly. Despite Brad's involvement, she thought this work project would be just what she needed. It would provide a distraction from the intensity of her job and the physical exercise would be invigorating. How could anyone resist the chance to work on a summer camp for kids—certainly she could not.

"Hello, Stacie."

Stacie was jolted out of her musings by the sound of Brad's voice. Instinctively she looked around for Megan, who had her back turned. She felt awkward, but there was no way out.

"Hello, Brad." Scrambling for something to ease the tension she suddenly felt, she offered, "I saw your new van; things must be going well."

"Yes, the business is going well; there is plenty of work for all of us." As always, Brad's tone was even and controlled, and, without hesitation, he looked directly into Stacie's eyes.

"I'm glad. I know how your men depend on you." It was not for his own sake alone that Brad was reluctant to leave

St. Mary's. He had three people working for him full-time who would lose their jobs if he closed his business.

Brad nodded. "This is a busy time of the year, you know, getting ready for the summer. When the nice weather gets here, we'll be swamped."

"Are you sure you have time for the work at the camp?" Stacie asked, half hoping that he would answer negatively.

"I'm sure I'll have some very long days, but I really want to do this."

"Me too." For a fleeting moment, Stacie wondered if Brad was also looking for a distraction. *Was it really feasible for them both to be involved in the same work project? Was it as hard for him to be together as it was for her?*

Their conversation seemed to have come to an awkward end, and Stacie wished Megan would hurry.

"Stacie. . . ." Brad moved a step closer. "Stacie, I miss you. . . . Couldn't we talk some more about this? If there's any chance you'll change your mind. . . ."

"It's not that simple, Brad," she said, looking away. She wanted desperately to step back from him, but she was already leaning against the wall and had nowhere to go.

"I can make a good living for us here, Stace, and you'd be free to get involved in any social projects you want. It wouldn't even matter if you got paid. Wouldn't that make you happy?" Brad was gently stroking her forearm with one finger, and she was tortuously tempted to look at his pleading face and surrender in agreement to what he offered. Nonchalantly, she moved her arm out of his reach and took a small step to the side.

"Brad, I miss you, too." She still avoided looking at his face. "I don't understand what's happening any more than you do, but I know God wants me to take this job." She spoke with conviction in her voice because she felt it in her heart.

"It doesn't have to be this way, Stacie."

"I don't have any choice, Brad."

"Ready to go?" Megan's lighthearted voice was a welcome interruption.

"Whenever you are," Stacie answered, turning toward Megan and giving Brad a clear signal that their conversation was over.

"I'm sorry about that," Megan said when they got outside the building. "I said I wouldn't leave your side, and then off I went the first time someone called my name."

"It's okay, Megan." It was drizzling again, and Stacie pulled the hood of her jacket up over her head. "After all, you can't run interference between Brad and me indefinitely. It's been two months since we broke up.

"What did he want?" She unlocked the car and they got in.

"He wants me to change my mind."

"Why doesn't he change his mind?" Megan asked innocently as she turned the key in the ignition.

Stacie shrugged, "He's got good reasons, sensible reasons. Brad has a thriving business with people who depend on him, and I just have a dinky, little, nonprofit job."

"Don't talk that way!" Megan said sharply, and then added more softly, "Your reasons for going to Thomasville are just as good as his reasons for staying in St. Mary's."

Stacie appreciated Megan's support. Most people could not understand why Stacie would give up Brad for the job in Thomasville, and she seemed unable to make them understand that it was not a choice she wanted to make. Megan, however, understood that Stacie simply could not make the obvious, easy decision unless she was convinced it was also the right decision. They drove several blocks in silence and pulled up in front of Stacie's apartment.

"Are we still playing tennis on Sunday afternoon?" Megan asked.

"Sure, if the rain stops," Stacie answered. "The forecast calls for rain all weekend."

"Well, if you don't play you can always come over and help me clean out my refrigerator instead," said Megan.

Stacie laughed. The chaos of Megan's refrigerator had been a standing joke between them for more than a year, and the simple reference to it conjured up reassurances of the depth and solidity of their friendship.

Stacie let herself into her apartment and reached for the light switch. With her fingers poised to flick it on, she changed her mind and set her things down in the dark. Her feet took the familiar path to the couch where she stretched out and stared up at the shadows on the ceiling.

Could Brad be right? she wondered. *Am I misunderstanding what God is saying to me just because this job is what I've always wanted? After all, Brad is what I've always wanted, too, and what he says makes a lot of sense. How can I be so sure about two things that are completely incompatible with each other? Is this some kind of a test?*

She lay in the dark for a long time. Obviously, there were no easy answers, and she struggled with the polarity of her emotions until she lapsed into an exhausted sleep. It was several hours later when she roused herself and moved to the bed for the rest of the night. All too soon the alarm clock was buzzing once again.

three

"Hey Stacie! The doughnuts are here."

It was a Friday morning ritual at the office: enormous frosted doughnuts from the Swedish bakery across the street and freshly brewed, raspberry cream gourmet coffee. Today's goodies were supplied by Marsha, the receptionist.

Stacie put down her pencil and looked up from the report she had been immersed in for the last two hours. It was not very interesting reading, but the report had been issued by the governor's office and she had to know what it was about. Why couldn't government people write in plain English? she always wondered. How could their programs ever work if nobody could understand them? Even though she was not in the mood to socialize, she decided she would go have a doughnut; maybe the break would perk her up a little bit.

The little room the agency used for breaks and lunch was already full. Friday, when there were doughnuts, was the one day of the week that everyone managed to get away from their desks for a few minutes in the morning. Glancing around, Stacie saw that she was the last staff member to arrive.

"There are still three doughnuts left," Marsha said, pointing to the top of the filing cabinet where the box sat. "You were a little too pokey this morning."

Stacie smiled and inspected the open box. Three golden, glazed doughnuts lay flat in the bottom, daring her to select just one. She picked up a doughnut with one hand and a napkin with the other and turned around to look for a place to sit. Marsha motioned to an empty chair next to her; Stacie complied and sat down beside the stout, middle-aged woman who colored her hair a very strange shade of orange.

"Are you making any progress with that report?" Marsha got the question out just before filling her mouth with another bite.

"Slowly but surely," Stacie said. "There is a lot of good information in it, but it's hidden behind a pile of words that don't really mean much." She took a careful bite of her doughnut, trying not to get a ring of glaze around her mouth.

Marsha was licking her fingers now. "Well, you've got the circles under your eyes to prove that you've been trying to read it." She smiled slyly at Stacie. "Or did you have one of your wild nights last night?"

To Marsha, who lived alone with her three cats and went to bed at 9:00 every evening, anyone who didn't go straight home from work every night and stay there until morning was having a wild time. In Stacie's mind, going to a Bible study at the church was hardly having a wild night, but she merely smiled and let Marsha continue with her fantasy of what Stacie's life was like. She got up and poured herself a cup of steaming coffee and took a cautious sip. "Mmm, I like this flavor, Marsha," she said.

"You say that every time I get it."

"That's because I like it every time." Stacie took another bite of her doughnut. "Is it my turn to buy next week?"

"Check the schedule by the water cooler," Marsha directed.

"I'll do that." Stacie took her doughnut and coffee and started back to her office.

"Oh!" Marsha's tone made Stacie turn around and look, questioningly. "I forgot to tell you. When Jack was here for

his coffee he was looking for you. You should probably
check with him. I don't know what he wanted."

"Thanks, Marsha. I'll check it out."

Stacie normally met with the agency's director on
Wednesday afternoons and their last meeting had been routine. She wondered why he would be looking for her on a
Friday morning. The first thing she had to do was finish the
doughnut and clean up her sticky fingers. She crammed the
last of the pastry into her mouth just as she sat down in her
chair. In the middle of her desk was a note from Jack Rogers
that had not been there when she left a few minutes ago. The
note said he wanted to see her.

With her napkin, she dabbed at the corners of her mouth
and wiped her fingertips. From the center desk drawer she
pulled out a small mirror and looked at her image. The
evidence of the doughnut was gone, but Marsha was right
about the circles under her eyes. If only Marsha knew the
truth of what Stacie's life was like right now, she might not
make those frequent remarks about wild nights.

Standing up, she straightened her skirt and brushed
crumbs off the sleeve of her blouse. Jack wanted to see her
right away; no matter how tired she was, there was no point
in putting it off. Stacie went to the end of the short hall,
turned right, and knocked on the first office door.

"Come in!" said a voice.

She turned the knob and pushed the door open. "You
wanted to see me?"

"Yes, Stacie, come on in." Jack Rogers motioned for her to
sit in one of the blue chairs across from his woodgrain desk.
As always, his office was immaculate and meticulously neat.
Each file folder had its proper place, every book was on the
right shelf, and the trash can was neatly tucked out of sight.

Whenever Stacie went to Jack's office, she felt guilty for the clutter that characterized hers. At thirty-five, Jack had a lot of responsibility and was obsessively productive; he also managed to be very tidy about everything he did.

"I just read your last memo," Jack said as Stacie got settled in the chair. "You've got some great ideas for the new shelter. It's obvious you've put a lot of energy into your thinking."

Stacie was grateful for the compliment but felt awkward receiving it. "The project is an important one," she said, taking the focus off herself.

"It's time to get some numbers together. We'll have to restructure the inside of the building we have and we need to know what that's going to cost." Jack tapped the end of his pencil on the edge of the desk. "I think it would be good if you went to Thomasville next week. Have you met the director you'll be working with?"

Stacie shook her head. "I've seen some of his correspondence, and we've spoken on the phone once, but I haven't met him in person."

"Dillon Graves is a good guy. You'll like him. Very capable." Jack swiveled his chair and leaned back thoughtfully. "I'll ask Marsha to check with him about his schedule. Maybe you can work something out for the end of next week. The two of you can go through the building together and sketch out how you think it should be arranged. Then we can get estimates from local contractors and go from there."

Stacie nodded. "Sounds good. I don't see a problem." She stood up to leave.

Jack reached back to the credenza behind him and picked up two large computer reports. Pushing them across the desk toward Stacie, he said, "I know these are no fun, but you'd better look at these when you're done with the one you have." He smiled at her. "Speaking of contractors, I ran into that friend of yours. Bill—is that his name?"

Stacie's heart started to beat faster. "Brad."

"That's right, Brad. Didn't I meet him at the Christmas party?"

"Yes, we came together." Stacie was nearly choking on the words.

"Nice guy. Too bad he doesn't live in Thomasville. We could use him there."

Not wanting to stand there and talk about Brad, Stacie picked up the reports and said brightly, "I'd better get my nose back to the grindstone."

Stacie let the heavy reports fall with a thud to her desk top—which did not look anything like Jack's. There were many things about Jack that Stacie admired. He was very efficient, understood the seriousness of the problems he faced every day, and dealt fairly with his staff. But, for a person whose job was to help people, Jack Rogers had an incredible capacity to ignore the personal lives of the people he was with the most. When Jack met Brad last Christmas, it was common knowledge that Stacie was engaged to him— even Jack knew what the diamond on her left hand meant. Now, he did not remember Brad's name and called him "that friend of yours."

Jack's confidence in her as an assistant director meant a lot to Stacie. But now she realized that he had no idea what price she was paying to accept the position he offered. She wondered if it had ever even crossed his mind that her engagement might complicate her decision about the new job. Hadn't he even wondered what happened to Brad?

The new reports would have to wait until she finished

plowing through the one she had left open on her desk. With a soft groan, she picked them up and looked around for a better place to put them. There was an open spot on the top of the bookcase, so she put them there. Has Jack always been so neat, she wondered, or is it only because he has a big office?

She had never had a chance to finish her raspberry creme gourmet coffee, and now it was cold. Stacie thought about going back to the break room to see if there was any hot coffee left but decided against it. She still had more than eighty pages to get through before the end of the day.

Her phone rang. She picked it up and said mechanically, "Stacie Hanaken."

"Don't sound so excited," the voice said facetiously.

"Hi, Megan. It's been a hard day, that's all."

"More government reports?"

"Right. Reading this stuff is like chewing sand."

"Let me make you a better offer. Let's go to Katie's Kitchen for dinner. My treat."

"Oh, I don't know, Megan. I'm pretty tired."

"Come on, Stace," Megan pleaded. "I don't want you going home and having soup from your freezer again, and sitting there all alone for the whole evening."

"Soup is nutritious." Stacie defended her eating habits.

"So have soup at Katie's Kitchen. Just get out of your apartment tonight." Megan sounded insistent, so Stacie relented.

"All right, we've got a date."

"This is a great table," Megan remarked, looking around. "It's away from the kitchen and sort of out of the way. I like it." The table for two was set with a crisp, crimson tablecloth and matching napkins. A low, burning candle glowed softly in the center of the table, next to a slender vase holding one rose.

Stacie hung her purse on her chair and sat down across from Megan. "I haven't been here too often. I like all the plants."

"I'm surprised you haven't been here more. It strikes me as the kind of atmosphere you would really like. And the food is great."

Stacie looked at the wall behind Megan and nodded. Throughout the restaurant there were pictures of historic Victorian houses, each of which was matted in soft blues and pinks and framed in oak.

"You're right. I do like it. I always have. But Brad didn't care for this place very much. . . ."

"Oh." Megan did not need to use a lot of words to let Stacie know she understood.

Stacie changed the subject. "I kill everything I bring into my apartment. I hope that my being this close to all these gorgeous plants won't hurt them!"

Megan chuckled. "You were never any good at basic science. Plants need water, my friend. You always forget that."

To her own surprise, Stacie found herself laughing, too. "Maybe I should visit your kindergarten class the next time you have that plant-a-seed-and-see-what-happens project.

A wide shadow crept across their table and their bantering came to a halt. "Good evening, ladies," said a dour woman whose face was surrounded by wisps of grayish hair that had come loose from her ponytail. She hardly moved her mouth as she delivered her dry, unenthusiastic speech: "My name is Rita, and I'll be your server tonight. Here are your menus. The specials are marked on the back. I'll be back in a few minutes to take your order." As she slapped the menus down on the table and disappeared, Megan and Stacie laughed even harder.

Rita was back almost immediately; Stacie and Megan had barely recovered their composure enough to tell her what they wanted to eat. She set a basket of warm rolls between them and left just as abruptly as the last time.

In spite of Rita's making it known that she was having a very bad day, Megan and Stacie were enjoying themselves. It had been a long time since they had been out to dinner together, and they found it as pleasant as it always had been. They sipped their iced teas and generously spread real butter on their homemade rolls.

"This is so naughty," Stacie said, eyeing the warm roll in her hand as the butter was starting to drip down toward her wrist. "You should have seen the doughnut I had at work this morning."

"Aw, live it up for once," Megan said. "There's always next week for dieting." She took an enthusiastic bite of her own roll.

"Speaking of next week, Jack Rogers wants to send me to Thomasville. I'm supposed to meet—" Stacie broke off abruptly.

"Stace? What's the matter? Are you all right?"

Stacie forced herself to swallow. "I'm fine, Megan." She took a sip of her tea. "No, I'm not fine, Megan. Don't turn around, but Brad just walked in."

Megan's eyebrows moved together in a puzzled look. "I thought you said he didn't like this place."

Stacie nodded. "That's what he always told me. But he's not alone, and maybe *she* is more persuasive than I am."

Megan was fidgeting in her chair, working very hard at not

turning around to stare. "She who? Who is he with?"

"Jenna."

"Jenna!" Megan was appalled. "Brad came here with Jenna McLean? She can't be more than nineteen years old."

"She's a nice girl, actually."

"Come on, Stacie, you don't have to say things like that to me. How could he give up someone like you to go out with Jenna McLean?"

"We broke up, Megan. I have no claim on Brad."

"Has he spotted us?"

Stacie shook her head. "I can see him through the branches of that rubber plant behind you but I don't think he can see us."

"Do you want to leave?" Megan prodded.

Stacie thought for a second and then said, "No, we've already ordered. Besides, we would have to walk right past them to get to the door."

"You don't have to put yourself through this, Stace. We can go eat soup at your place if you want."

"I want to stay, Megan," Stacie said definitively. "Let's change the subject. Tell me what you know about this camp we're going to be working at."

"Well, I went there two summers in a row when I was in grade school. I remember it as being a pretty neat place to go."

"Were the Barrowses there?"

"Yes, and they seemed ancient then," said Megan. "I can only imagine what Mrs. Barrows must look like now."

"To a kid, everyone is old. Maybe she wasn't as old as you thought."

"Maybe. I can remember. . . ."

Stacie heard very little of what Megan said for the next

few minutes. The branches and leaves of the rubber plant were spaced perfectly for her to discretely view Brad and Jenna across the room. She simply did not have enough will power to stop watching the two of them, with their heads leaning close together over one menu and shy smiles passing between them. Jenna tossed her head, laughing at something Brad said, and her blond, wavy hair floated gracefully through the air and settled back on her shoulders. With a demure smile, she reached out and laid her hand lightly on Brad's forearm. He responded by placing his other hand over hers and looking directly at Jenna with a wide smile on his face.

Stacie could see their lips moving in a conversation which obviously delighted them both. It was unlikely that they would notice her, tucked away at a secluded little table. In fact, they seemed so completely absorbed in each other that they were noticing very little of what happened around them.

Brad tipped his head back in laughter again and then lightly thumped Jenna's upturned nose with his forefinger, before leaning over to kiss her.

"Stacie? Stace, are you all right?" Megan's voice pulled Stacie out of the fog she felt swirling around her. "You look pale, Stacie. Are you feeling all right?"

"I'm okay," Stacie answered, in a whisper.

Megan twisted in her chair and looked through the leaves of the rubber plant. It took her only a moment to know what was upsetting Stacie. "Have you been watching them?" she scolded.

"I couldn't help it," Stacie answered pitifully. "We broke up. There's no reason he shouldn't go out with whomever he wants. But I can't help feeling jealous. The way he is with her—that's the way we used to be together." Stacie's eyes were filling with tears. "Maybe you and I should trade places so I'll have my back to them."

"I have a better idea," Megan said determinedly. "When that waitress with the sparkling personality gets back, we'll tell her we want our food to go."

"Don't be ridiculous, Megan. We came here to eat, so we'll eat."

"Don't give me an argument, Stacie. You always do things the hard way. You don't have to put yourself through this. We're leaving."

A few minutes later, Megan guided Stacie's elbow right past Brad and Jenna's table without stopping, and without even looking at them. Whether Brad saw her or not, Stacie did not know.

four

Megan eased her small car down the narrow road and followed the circle around until she came to a stop in front of a small stone cottage. "It sure looks different from what I remember," she said to Stacie, her only passenger. Looking around, they could see that they were the first of the church group to arrive at the camp.

Stacie glanced at her watch: 9:37 A.M. "We're early. What do you think we should do?"

"We could see if Mrs. Barrows is in the house, or we could just get out and look around." Megan opened her door and stuck her head out. "At least it stopped raining."

They got out and surveyed their surroundings. The cottage was about twenty feet ahead of them. Paint was peeling off the black shutters, and the flower beds were overgrown with a tangled mess of weeds. The walk leading to the house had large gaps where the stones had given way to the soft mud and sunk several inches into the ground.

"Are you sure this is where she lives?" Stacie was doubtful. "It's hard to tell if anyone is here."

"From what I remember, this is the place." Megan turned and looked in the other direction. "We used to play softball in that field over there. It looks like an enormous weed patch now. And, if you follow the road around the circle a little farther, you get to the cabins, girls on one side of the road, boys on the other." Megan gestured to a small dilapidated shed behind the house. "There used to be some equipment stored in there."

Stacie inspected the dubious building from a distance. "If all the buildings look like that, we have our work cut out for us." One wall had definitely separated from the roof, and the glass in the single window had been shattered. The wood around the door frame was half-rotted, making Stacie think the shed would collapse if anyone unknowingly leaned against it. She turned her attention back to the house. "Should we ring the bell or wait for the others to get here?"

"We might as well let her know we're here. Maybe we can get started on something." Megan gingerly led the way along the mud and stone path and rang the bell.

Almost immediately the door opened. "Come on in, girls. I heard your car pull up." Margaret Barrows took Stacie by the wrist and literally pulled her into the cottage. Her grip was firm and her smile sincere.

Somehow Stacie thought an elderly, widowed woman would be small and frail, but Margaret Barrows was five feet, eight inches tall and looked robust. One shoulder hunched slightly as she moved quickly around on her long legs. Her gray, curly hair framed a face with wide cheekbones, and silver glasses highlighted her blue eyes.

"Please, sit down," Mrs. Barrows said. "I'll get you some juice."

Megan protested. "No, please, we don't want you to go to any trouble. We know we're early, but the others will be here soon, I'm sure."

"I'm sure they will, dear." Mrs. Barrows smiled indulgently at both Megan and Stacie. "But until they arrive, you just sit down and make yourselves comfortable. I'll be right back." She disappeared through a swinging door and Megan and Stacie were left standing awkwardly in the living room.

Stacie shrugged her shoulders. "I guess we should sit down. She means business about the juice."

Megan smiled and relaxed. "Okay. She's the boss."

They sat side by side on the couch and found themselves looking across the room at a wall filled with framed photographs. Many of the pictures were black and white. Quite a few were poses of happy, smiling campers from over the years; others were of family members, Stacie supposed. One face appeared over and over again, and she felt as if she were watching a young man age gradually as her eyes moved from the left side of the wall to the far right. Obviously, he was someone important to Mrs. Barrows.

"You have quite a collection of photographs," Stacie said when Mrs. Barrows come back into the room.

"Every face up there is special." Mrs. Barrows set a tray down on the coffee table in front of Megan and Stacie. Two tall glasses were filled with ice cubes and apple juice, and there was a plate laden with bran muffins and banana bread. "I thought maybe you'd be hungry, too."

Stacie and Megan looked at each other and smiled, silently wondering what to make of Margaret Barrows.

"David always liked to have banana bread around," Mrs. Barrows explained. "I can't seem to break the habit of making some every week."

"David was your husband?" Megan ventured.

"For sixty years." Mrs. Barrows looked fondly at the last photo on the wall. "That one was taken before he got so sick." She gestured toward the tray. "Please, help yourselves to something to eat."

Stacie obediently reached for a slice of banana bread; Megan chose a muffin. Contented, Mrs. Barrows lowered herself into a recliner across from them. "Tell me about yourselves. I don't even know your names."

This put Stacie and Megan at ease, and, in between bites of delicious, home-baked bread, they did not hesitate to tell their hostess about their jobs and interests. Megan was in the middle of an outrageously funny story about one of her kindergarteners when they heard the sound of cars pulling up in front of the house.

"Looks like the rest of the crew is here." Mrs. Barrows stood up and went to the window. Stacie and Megan were right behind her.

"That looks like everybody," Stacie said. Including the two of them, there were nine volunteers from the group who had come to spend the day working. From the grubby way they were dressed, no one would have ever guessed the responsible, professional jobs that most of them held. Brad had come in his new van. He dropped down from the driver's seat and went around to the other side of the van to open the door. Before Stacie could even see who it was that had come with Brad, she knew it was Jenna McLean. Stacie sighed as quietly as she could. This was going to be harder than she thought.

Mrs. Barrows was already out the front door and striding across the weedy lawn toward the motley-looking group. Enthusiastically, she shook the hand of everyone who had come.

Megan took one last swallow of apple juice and said, "We'd better get out there before all the good jobs are gone." Reluctantly, Stacie followed her outside.

Mrs. Barrows was already in the middle of her exuberant instructions. "I have plenty of buckets and brushes for scrubbing the insides of the cabins. That shed behind the house has a couple of lawn mowers in it. If you can't find the gasoline, let me know, it might be in the basement. There should be a weed trimmer in there, too. If you need water, there is a big reel of hose around the side of the house."

Stacie could not help but smile at the contagious enthusiasm of Mrs. Barrows. It was obvious she had a good idea of what needed to be done and was well prepared for the work crew.

Megan nudged Stacie's elbow. "Can you believe her?" she whispered. "Most people her age would be happy just to settle back and enjoy their retirement. It's incredible that she has the energy to get this place going again."

Stacie nodded. "It'll be great when it's all done."

Mrs. Barrows clapped her hands sharply. "Okay folks. Let's get to it!"

Soft laughter rippled through the group, but they immediately complied. Brad and a couple of the other men headed for the shed to see about the lawn mowers. Several of the women started unwinding the long hose so that the buckets could be filled. Stacie stood still for a moment, unable to fight the habit of watching Brad as he walked away. A slight movement in her peripheral vision caught her attention, and she realized she was not the only one watching Brad. Jenna was standing right where Brad had left her.

Stacie immediately moved into action. Since Brad was apparently going to work on cutting the grass she would simply opt for an indoor job, and she probably would not run into him all day. Maybe Jenna would stay outside, too. She snatched up a bucket and headed for the water hose. Megan and Mrs. Barrows were already walking side by side toward the first of the cabins and Stacie decided to join them. She squirted some soap into the bottom of the bucket, squeezed the nozzle of the hose to fill it, and followed the others around the circle road.

The inside of the cabin was musty with layers of dust. Mrs. Barrows produced a broom from one corner and batted at the cobwebs hanging from the ceiling. Megan managed to pry open the windows and found a rock to prop open the door so the fresh air could circulate. Stacie pushed up the sleeves of her oldest sweatshirt, gripped a brush, and plunged her arm into the soapy water. The others had gone to work on the next cabin up the road, so Megan, Stacie, and Mrs. Barrows were on their own.

The day passed more quickly than Stacie had expected. After a couple of hours, everyone stopped for a quick picnic lunch and then got right back to work. By the middle of the afternoon, Megan, Stacie, and Mrs. Barrows were able to move on to another cabin to begin the process all over again.

Mrs. Barrows was very appealing, Stacie decided. She was not the doting grandmotherly type that Stacie had expected. It was true that Margaret talked a lot, but it was fun to listen to her stories about the campers she had known over the years. When she found out that Megan had been to the camp as a child, Mrs. Barrows squealed with delight and launched into a whole new set of stories from Megan's era. More than once, Stacie and Megan had to put their brushes down and compose themselves to keep from collapsing with laughter.

"Knock, knock." Stifling their giggles, the three of them turned to see Brad standing in the doorway. Stacie had not seen him since that morning.

"I don't mean to interrupt your fun," he said with a sparkle in his eyes, "but Donna wants to talk to Megan." He looked directly at Megan now. "She wondered if you could come out to where she's working."

"Sure." Megan plopped her brush in her bucket and wiped her hands on her jeans. "It's probably about Sunday School tomorrow. I said I would take her class."

Brad stepped aside to let Megan through the door, but he made no move to leave himself.

Out of the corner of her eye, Stacie tracked Brad. She dipped her brush in the water again and vigorously attacked the dirty wall in front of her. Gray water spattered back at her face, making her blink involuntarily, but she kept at her task, rubbing the wall as hard as she could. With the bright sky behind him, Brad's muscular form stood silhouetted in the doorway.

Mrs. Barrows picked up her bucket and moved it farther down the wall. "Pretty soon we'll need clean water, Stacie."

"Yes, I suppose so," muttered Stacie without looking at either the water or Mrs. Barrows, but only at the wall. Her elbows bobbed up and down with her effort.

"I'll just go get some right now." Mrs. Barrows dropped her brush and bent over to grip the bucket handle with both hands.

"Please, let me go," Stacie offered, politely. *Oh, please let me go!* her mind screamed.

"Nonsense, I can manage just fine. I'll be right back."

She was gone. There was no one to shield Stacie from Brad, who had moved to let Mrs. Barrows pass and then stepped into the cabin instead of out, as Stacie had hoped.

Brad turned his head from side to side. "Looks like you're making good progress in here."

"Yes, I think we are."

"The lawn is almost under control out there."

"That's good."

"I understand there's another set of cabins, too."

"So Megan told me." Stacie wished Brad would leave, so she certainly was not going to encourage any conversation with him.

But Brad was not easily dissuaded. He walked over to the window and knocked on the loose frame. "Looks like I'd better put this on my list of things to fix."

Stacie scrubbed even harder and wondered how long Mrs. Barrows would be gone.

"That beam doesn't look too secure, either." Brad looked up at the ceiling above Stacie's head. He was behind her now, so she could not see him, but she could sense him, and she knew he was coming closer. Casually she stepped to the side and started scrubbing a new spot.

"Can't you even talk to me, Stacie?" She knew Brad was trying to get her to look at him, and she refused.

"Here we go, clean water." Finally, Mrs. Barrows was back. "I put extra soap in it this time, too. Maybe that will speed things up."

Stacie forced herself to brighten up. "I'm sure it will. We'll be done soon, anyway." She stepped away from Brad and took the bucket from Mrs. Barrows. She jostled it just a little, and the water sloshed over the side and left a soapy puddle at her feet. Keeping her distance from Brad in a way that she hoped would give him a clear signal, she set the bucket down and resumed her work.

"Mrs. Barrows, I see some things that need fixing around here," Brad said. "Maybe I'll take a look at all the cabins and make one master list of what needs to be done."

"Oh, that would be wonderful, Brad." Mrs. Barrows was more than pleased at Brad's suggestion. "David used to take care of all the building problems. I'm afraid I'm not much use in that department."

"Well, don't worry about it," Brad reassured her. "I'll make sure everything is in tiptop shape." He smiled at Mrs. Barrows and looked over at Stacie. "I suppose I'd better get back outside. Just let me know if there is anything I can do for you, Mrs. Barrows."

"What you're already doing is wonderful, all of you. How can I tell you how much I appreciate it?"

"We're glad to help." Brad wiggled his fingers in a goodbye wave and left.

Once he was gone, Stacie slowed her scrubbing speed considerably and started breathing more deeply. Mrs. Barrows wordlessly picked up her own brush and also started in again. All day long they had bantered back and forth and laughed until their sides hurt. The quiet between them now felt very strange to Stacie, but she didn't know what to say. After a few minutes, Mrs. Barrows broke the silence.

"Are you and Brad friends?"

"Sure," Stacie answered quickly—perhaps too quickly. "We're all friends; everyone in the group likes to be together."

Mrs. Barrows scratched at a stubborn spot on the wall. "You didn't say a word to Brad. I got the feeling that you didn't even want to be here with him."

Stacie did not answer. She could not; the words just did not come.

"Maybe we should take a break, Stacie," Mrs. Barrows said gently.

"No, I'm fine. We'll be done before too long." Stacie started scrubbing harder again.

Mrs. Barrows put her hand over Stacie's and took hold of

the brush. "I insist. The dirt has been here a long time; a few more minutes won't make a difference. Let's go up to the cottage and have tea."

Stacie didn't have the strength to argue.

Once again Stacie found herself in the quaint living room gazing at the wall of pictures. Mrs. Barrows swooped up the tray Stacie and Megan had left that morning and vanished into the kitchen. In a few minutes, Stacie heard the comforting whistle of the teakettle and knew that she would have only a few more minutes alone. It was obvious that Mrs. Barrows had detected something was wrong, even though she had known Stacie for less than a day. The question now was, how much should Stacie tell her?

"Here we go. I brought sugar and lemon so you can fix your tea just the way you like it. We should probably let it steep for a few more minutes."

Stacie was admiring the white porcelain teapot with a pattern of blue windmills. "What a beautiful teapot," she said sincerely. "The windmills look so delicate, and there's so much detail."

"David gave me that for our fortieth wedding anniversary."

"It's a beautiful gift. It sounds like he was a thoughtful husband."

Mrs. Barrows tilted her head and smiled. "We had our tough times, but he was a good man. I was very happy being married to him."

Stacie felt a lump forming in her throat. She had hoped to say something like that about Brad someday, but now she did not know if she would ever feel that way about any man.

"When I think of how close I came to not marrying David. . . ." Mrs. Barrows shook her head.

The question hung in the air, so Stacie had to ask it. "What do you mean? Did you have doubts about whether you should get married?"

"It's a long story, but there was another young man before David. I was very young, and there were a bunch of us who ran around together. I was madly in love with one of the boys before I met my husband. But David—David was in a class by himself—and there was a spark between us right from the start. Still, I felt a sense of loyalty to Henry. When he asked me to marry him, I said yes, and convinced myself that what I felt for David was just puppy love and I would get over it. When I think of what I would have missed if I had not married David . . . let's just say I'm awfully glad I did."

Stacie's eyes were filled with tears, and she could barely hold back the sobs.

Mrs. Barrows poured a cup of tea and handed it to Stacie. "Now, dear, why don't you tell me just what is going on between you and Brad."

five

The view outside the window was a shapeless rush of colors as the train rumbled down tracks that had been in use for half a century. For a midwestern spring, the day was fairly bright. Every now and then, when the train slowed down enough, Stacie could see flecks of green dancing on the brown branches and knew that the spring rains were doing their work. April would be brighter and more colorful than March had been and spring would burst forth with its yearly reminder of the wonder of life.

Stacie had anticipated leisurely enjoying the countryside from the comfort of her reclined seat on the train. But she had not expected the lulling sensation brought on by the steady motion of the train and, after the first fifty miles, she found herself struggling to stay alert. She knew she needed to rest because she had not been sleeping well. Still, she felt she ought to be doing something more productive with her time, even on a train.

When Jack Rogers first suggested that Stacie should take a trip to Thomasville, she assumed she would drive the 200 miles to her future home. When Megan made a casual comment about a childhood train ride, Stacie remembered that the railroad still operated a regular schedule between St. Mary's and Thomasville. Impulsively, and not characteristically, she called Dillon Graves to ask him to meet her at the train station.

Stacie forced herself to sit upright in her seat and took a professional magazine out of her briefcase. For a few moments she successfully concentrated on the lead article, but her mind began to wander. Although more awake now, it was still very hard for her to focus her thoughts. The photograph on the page in front of her blurred and somehow transformed itself into a picture of Mrs. Barrows, with her soft gray curls and bright eyes, handing Stacie a cup of steaming tea.

Even though she had known Margaret Barrows for only a few hours last Saturday afternoon, Stacie had unplugged her emotional dam and, while they shared a pot of tea, confided the whole story of her relationship with Brad. After spending so much of the day laughing with the older woman, Stacie took comfort in also sharing her tears. Now it was Thursday, and Stacie was plodding her way through her problems in the real world. Although talking with Mrs. Barrows had not given Stacie any immediate answers about her feelings for Brad, she had begun to feel less like an emotional blob and a little more like her old self.

As the train rocked rhythmically back and forth, Stacie turned the page of the magazine and made another stab at reading. The article was about a new program for developmentally disabled children in a suburb of Chicago, and for more than a week Stacie had been looking forward to having time to read the entire article. One paragraph at a time, she made her way through the description of the unique program, with its advantages and disadvantages.

"Next stop, Thomasville." The conductor's garbled voice barely came through the static of the speaker at the front of the car, but Stacie already knew that they were getting close to the station in Thomasville. She closed her magazine and put it back into her briefcase, then laid her head back to look out the window and enjoy the last few minutes of the scenery.

To Stacie, Dillon Graves was only a voice on the phone or a signature at the bottom of a letter. She had never even seen a photograph of him, so she did not really know who she was looking for when she got off the train and scanned the old wooden platform. It was the middle of the day when she arrived and there were not many people around, so she thought surely it would be obvious who Dillon Graves was. One man sat on a bench reading a newspaper; he did not even look up when the passengers stepped off the train, so obviously he was not Dillon. The only other man she saw looked much too old; Jack had said that Dillon was thirty-two.

Stacie picked up her small suitcase and decided to go inside the station; it was empty except for the ticket agent. Trying to look hopeful but wondering if she had made a mistake, Stacie found a wooden bench that looked fairly clean and tentatively sat down.

"Stacie?"

She jumped at the sound of a smooth voice over her shoulder. Fumbling with her briefcase, she said, "Yes, I'm Stacie. You're Dillon?"

"That's me." He smiled at her and put out his hand.

Stacie stood up and shook the soft hand of Dillon Graves. He was tall, several inches taller than she had imagined, with tightly-curled blondish hair which was boyishly long in the back. He wore clean but faded jeans and a beige tweed jacket over a yellow shirt which was open at the neck. On his feet were well-worn sneakers. Stacie was awkwardly aware of the crisp linen jacket and pants she had chosen to wear that day; she felt drastically overdressed, compared to Dillon.

"Let me help you with your bag." Dillon reached down and picked up the small suitcase. "Is this all you have?" he asked, his lips turned up softly at the corners.

"Yes," Stacie answered. "I'm staying only until Sunday." Afraid she would stare at his freckled face, she tried not to look directly at him. His appearance and clothes—everything about Dillon was different from the professional, methodical administrator she had pictured. But she liked him instantly.

Dillon gestured toward the doorway. "There's a nice park near here. I thought we could get some meat and bread from the deli next door and have a little picnic while we get to know each other."

"I'd like that," Stacie said with enthusiasm. "I'm starving."

"Great. You wait here while I put your things in my car. I'll leave it parked; we can come back for it later."

Stacie watched Dillon's lanky strides as he went to the parking lot and his ten-year-old compact car that needed a paint job. He opened the back door and set her things inside. Even from a distance she could not help responding to his warmth. Although they had spoken on the phone several times, Dillon was brand new to Stacie. She liked the fact that he did not know about her personal life or history and felt that this was a chance to be anybody she wanted to be, to explore a fresh start in a new place.

"Ready?" he said when he got back to where she was standing.

"Absolutely."

She walked comfortably alongside of Dillon. When they came around the side of the station, Stacie saw what looked like the main street of the town. There were a few antique shops and specialty stores, several century-old, limestone buildings which housed the city offices, and the small park that Dillon had mentioned. Already Stacie liked Thomasville; it seemed quaint and tidy and appealing. She knew though that there must be another side to life in Thomasville, or the agency would not be setting up a homeless shelter there. But what she had seen so far she liked very much.

"Here's the deli." Dillon's voice interrupted her mental evaluation of the town. "What do you like to eat?"

"Oh, anything would be fine."

"Come on. You must have some preferences."

Stacie relaxed and smiled. "All right. I'd like roast beef on a hoagie roll."

"We should be able to manage that," Dillon said, pulling open the door and holding it for Stacie. "They make a mean German potato salad here, too."

"Sounds great."

Dillon ordered the sandwiches, salad, and soft drinks to go. When their lunch was ready, they took the sacks and crossed the street to the park. Just as they got situated and unpacked the food, the wind gusted and they grabbed their napkins and cups, just in time. Instinctively, Stacie pulled up the collar of her jacket.

"Are you cold?" Dillon asked. "We could go back to the deli and sit inside."

Stacie shook her head. "The sun feels good. It's been such a rainy spring at home . . . I would hate to miss out on such a pretty day." She took a bite of her sandwich, trying not to embarrass herself by dropping food on her lap.

Dillon sipped his drink. "How long have you lived in

St. Mary's?"

Stacie thought for a quick moment while she chewed. She decided she could answer that question without opening up the conversation to everything that had happened to her during her years in St. Mary's. "I've been there about five years," she said brightly. "I went to St. Mary's College and then was lucky enough to find a job that would let me stay there."

"Sounds like you like it a lot."

Stacie tilted her head thoughtfully. "I guess I really do. I'm going to miss it when I move here."

Dillon waved his hand down the main street. "This is a great town, too. You'll see."

"You seem pretty confident."

Dillon smiled that warm smile of his. "I guess I'm prejudiced. My family lived here when I was in high school and I've always loved it. When I had the chance to come back for this job, I couldn't pass it up." He picked up his sandwich and pondered where the next bite should be.

"Did you always want to be a social worker?" Stacie asked.

Dillon shook his head. "No. In college I wanted to be a psychologist. But somewhere along the line I decided that if people didn't have a safe place to live there wasn't much point in trying to help them handle their emotional problems. So I got involved with a couple of homeless shelters, first as a volunteer and then on the staff."

"And now you're here," Stacie summarized, "ready to open a whole new center. I'm sure your psychology background isn't wasted in a job where you have to deal with people all the time."

"It comes in handy," Dillon agreed. "I have run into some

real characters, but I'm sure you have, too."

"Jack said you already have a contract on a building," Stacie said. "Is that working out all right?"

Dillon swallowed a mouthful of roast beef and shook his head. "We've had some problems. It's a bit complicated because the building is owned jointly by several people, and we have to get them all to agree to the sale. But I'm hopeful. In fact, they've already given me a key. When we're done here, I'll take you over and show you around."

"One more bite." Stacie pushed the last of her potato salad into her mouth and started collecting sandwich wrappings and napkins. "Ready when you are."

They strolled back to Dillon's car, their conversation becoming increasingly excited as they talked enthusiastically about the new project they would be sharing. Stacie decided that, as much as she loved St. Mary's, moving on to a new place would be good for her. Away from everything that was familiar, she felt invigorated with the potential of what lay ahead of her. It was already clear that working with Dillon would be a comfortable distraction from what she was leaving behind. Getting the new shelter set up would be challenging and time consuming and she would have little time on her hands for wishing she were back in St. Mary's.

Dillon unlocked the door on the passenger side and let her in. When he was settled in the driver's seat and had pulled out of the parking lot, he started pointing out features of Thomasville. "Like a lot of midwestern towns, Thomasville was built up along the railroad so that it would be easy to get supplies in. But, by the turn of the century, it was clear that Thomasville would never be the booming metropolis the founders thought it would be."

"From what I've seen so far, it seems like a nice town,"

Stacie said. "Why is there a homeless problem here?"

"A lot of people have been asking that question. The most obvious answer is the high unemployment in surrounding rural areas, especially since the manufacturing plant outside of town shut down three years ago. Some of those people have never been able to find another job."

They rode in silence for a few minutes, each of them absorbed in thoughts of the seriousness of the problems they would encounter.

"Have you started looking for a place to live yet?" Dillon asked.

"No. I was hoping to get a few leads this weekend. But I still have plenty of time until I'm scheduled to move."

"I'll keep my eyes open for you. I found an apartment in a nice building for a reasonable rent." Dillon looked over at Stacie and added, "I'm just sorry there aren't any vacancies right now."

"Me, too," Stacie blurted out before she realized what she had said. She was caught off guard by his remark and regretted answering so quickly. She hardly knew Dillon Graves; why should she be sorry that she could not live in his apartment building? Yet she was.

"The building is just up in the next block," Dillon explained. "I have to warn you that it needs a lot of work. I don't suppose you know any trustworthy contractors."

Stacie looked up at Dillon abruptly. Why would he ask her if she knew any contractors? From his expression she decided that the question was sincere and merely professional. She shook her head and answered truthfully. "I'm afraid I don't know anyone around here."

"Well, I have a couple of leads, so I guess we'll start collecting bids."

Contractors. Until Dillon said that word, she had not thought of Brad all day; it would be too easy to fall into despondency about what she was sacrificing in order to come to Thomasville. Instead, she resolved to concentrate on the good things that awaited her here in this new place.

They parked on the street in front of the old wooden building and Dillon unlocked the front door, He held it open for her, and Stacie cautiously stepped over the threshold. The floor creaked and felt strangely soft.

"Are you sure this is safe?"

"I wouldn't have brought you here if it weren't," Dillon assured her. "It's already passed city inspection, and, once the improvements are made, you'll forget it ever looked like this."

"I can't see anything. Aren't there any windows?"

Dillon chuckled. "They've been boarded up for years. Unfortunately, the light switch is across the room."

Stacie felt the firm touch of his hand on her elbow as he guided her through the shadows. Obviously, Dillon knew exactly where he was going, and Stacie was surprised at how easy it was to trust him. She was also surprised at the pleasure she felt from such a simple gesture as his hand on her elbow. *Did it mean anything? Couldn't he have crossed the room by himself and turned on the lights? Was he looking for a reason to touch her? Or was it all her imagination?*

"Here we are." The switch clicked and the room filled with light. Dillon's hands were in his pockets. The moment—if there had been one—was gone.

"I think this will be the reception area, with the registration desk over here." Dillon paced around the room while he talked. "We'll widen the hallway back there that leads to the kitchen and dining room and have the sleeping rooms up-stairs. Full capacity will be about sixty-five people."

For the next two hours, Stacie attentively followed Dillon around the building soaking in the information he had already gathered and asking questions to decide how she could help. More than once he stopped in mid-sentence to ask what she thought about something, reminding her that as assistant director her opinions would be an important part of making decisions when the shelter was functioning.

When the tour ended, the afternoon was nearly gone. Dillon told Stacie that he had made several appointments with city officials for the next day, and he wanted her to come to the meetings with him. "We'll get our business taken care of, and then maybe we can find something fun to do on Saturday."

"That would be great," Stacie heard herself saying, as if it were someone else speaking the words.

"Unfortunately, I have a commitment tonight, or we could have dinner together," Dillon said apologetically.

"Don't worry about me," Stacie answered. "I brought plenty of work along with me." Once again she was not sure what he meant by his comment. *Had he wanted to have dinner together to talk more about remodeling the building? Or did he have something else in mind?*

"Then I'll just drop you off at your motel and come back for you at about nine tomorrow morning."

"That should be fine."

For supper, Stacie had soup and salad at the little coffee shop across the street from her motel. By then it was already dark and she did not want to be out walking alone. After her active day and the hours of Dillon's company, her small motel room seemed strangely quiet and still, and, for a few minutes, she sat motionless on the end of the bed expecting something, she didn't know what, to happen. She was used to being alone in her own apartment but alone in a motel room, she felt isolated and lonely. Luckily, she had brought plenty of work along with her, mostly things to read, so she would have no trouble passing the evening.

She decided to treat herself to a long hot bath before delving into a stack of journals and newsletters from other shelters. Stacie wished she had brought along some bubble bath to soak in. Still, it would be a luxury to relax in the tub without any deadline for when she had to get out. She piled her thick hair on top of her head and lowered herself into the bath. With her neck leaning against the back of the tub, she closed her eyes and gradually relaxed. In a matter of moments, she was very near sleep.

Stacie knew that she was not sleeping, but she was not really awake either. Behind her closed eyelids, discordant images crashed into each other: Brad renovating the new shelter; Dillon visiting her apartment in St. Mary's; Brad's long and gentle kiss on the night they broke their engagement; Dillon's mysterious grasp on her elbow as he steered her across the dark room; Megan's face rising through clouds and looking from Brad to Dillon and back again; Mrs. Barrows and her pots of tea and pictures of David lining the wall; dinner with Dillon at a fancy restaurant in the middle of the park; Brad tilting his head back in laughter at Jenna McLean's humor; living next door to Dillon; the pain in Brad's voice as he said "Can't you even look at me?"

Water splashed out of the tub and onto the floor as Stacie stood up abruptly. This bath was not turning out to be very relaxing after all. She dried herself off, got dressed for bed and sat on the end of the bed to consider the rest of the evening. After what had happened when she almost dozed off in the tub, she was hesitant to try sleeping; besides, it was too early to go to bed. But she knew she would not remember anything she read if she tried to work tonight. Restlessly, she flipped on the television, something she rarely did at home, but she was desperate tonight. Scanning the television guide, she reluctantly admitted that there was nothing on that she wanted to watch, so she shut the set off.

If Dillon had not had a commitment for this evening, she could be enjoying his company right this minute, relishing an interesting appetizer instead of fearing disturbing dreams. *Would she have gone to dinner with him*, she wondered, *if she believed that his interest was personal and not professional?* Five days ago she had told Mrs. Barrows that she still loved Brad; now she was wishing that Dillon had not dropped her off at her motel and gone on with his life. Those two facts simply did not make sense when placed side by side.

Something was wrong—or something was changing.

six

Stacie decisively pressed the print button on her desktop computer and sat back in her chair to relax for a few moments. For several weeks, ever since her trip to Thomasville, she had been spending a lot of her time trying to clear up projects that needed to be done before she could move. Jack Rogers told her not to worry about most of the things, but her own conscience demanded that she do her best to get everything done.

The laser printer, stationed outside her office door in the reception area, sucked another piece of paper through its mysterious insides, and clicked as it spit the page out the other end. Stacie listened for the familiar series of sounds three more times before getting up and going out to the printer to retrieve her report.

"Got a wild weekend planned?" Marsha popped her head out from behind her desk, a stack of folders on the corner of her desk nearly obscuring her.

Stacie shrugged. "Nothing too exciting. I'm going to spend Saturday out at the camp again."

"Haven't you been out there an awful lot lately?"

"It's been a couple of months since we started on the project," Stacie said, "but things are coming along."

"Are they going to be ready for campers this summer?"

"Absolutely. The owner hopes to start advertising soon, and camp can start before the end of June."

Stacie collected her report and ducked back into her office. Before she even sat down, Marsha was standing in the doorway. Stacie had not thought Marsha could move that fast.

"Almost forgot to tell you that Dillon Graves called while you were out to lunch."

Stacie looked up, her interest piqued. "Did he say what he wanted?"

"He asked to talk to Jack. Actually, he sounded upset." Her message relayed, Marsha turned and sauntered back to her chair.

Stacie had been in contact with Dillon several times a week ever since they met. She appreciated that he included her in decisions about setting up the office and the sleeping rooms and his cheerful voice on the phone was always a welcome interruption. After spending three days with him, he was no longer a faceless mystery; in fact, every time they spoke, she could picture his freckled face and crinkled smile.

Beyond that, she was unsure what to think of Dillon Graves. He had a face now, but he was still a mystery. When they were together, she almost believed that he was attracted to her and, to her own surprise, she responded warmly. But their contact in the weeks since their weekend visit had been strictly professional, and now Stacie thought she had probably been mistaken about him all along. Her dilemma was that she still felt herself responding to him personally. Relating to him about the work they had in common was comfortable, but she was curious about what it would be like to see him every day. Would it be easier to figure him out when they were working together, or would she still find herself wondering what he was thinking and feeling?

It was strange that Marsha said that Dillon sounded upset. Although Stacie had to admit that she did not know Dillon Graves very well, she had a hard time picturing him getting upset easily. Either Marsha was inferring something that was not there, or something drastic had happened; Stacie could not imagine what that could be.

The report now lay on the desk in front of her, waiting to be checked for mistakes. Stacie spread the four pages out across the desk and started reading slowly and carefully. She was halfway through the second page when she intuitively sensed someone in the doorway. It was Jack Rogers.

"What's wrong, Jack?" she asked, instantly knowing he was upset; Marsha must have been right about Dillon.

Jack closed the door behind him and sunk heavily into the faded gray chair against the wall across from her desk.

"Dillon called. The deal is off."

"What?" Stacie's mind churned faster than she could speak. "The shelter—doesn't Dillon want to run the new shelter?"

"The deal for the building is off," Jack clarified, pressing his lips together in disgust. "It's owned by a group of people and one of them doesn't want to sell. And the way their partnership is worded, that's all it takes to call the whole thing off."

Still in shock, Stacie did not know what to say. "But I thought we had a contract. . . ."

Jack shrugged. "It was contingent on the agreement of all parties concerned. And one party does not agree."

"Why not?"

"Who knows? Maybe she's not happy with the purchase price we agreed on; maybe she doesn't like the thought of destitute people wandering around her prestigious building; maybe she's on a power trip."

Stacie stared bleakly at her bookcase and the stack of resources she had already organized to take with her. "This is ridiculous." She forced out a heavy sigh. "What happens now?"

"Well, I've been on the phone all afternoon with several of the board members. The consensus is that we should go ahead and try to open a new shelter anyway. But it may not be in Thomasville."

"But Thomasville needs a shelter."

Jack nodded. "I know. But so do a lot of other places. Like Weston."

"Weston?"

"That was our second choice all along. One of the board members has a building that he can make available almost immediately."

"But what about approval from the city and all the homework that we've already done in Thomasville?" Stacie asked.

"We'll just have to do it all over again."

"Is Dillon willing to go to Weston?"

"I think so, Stacie. Are you?"

Weston was only thirty miles from St. Mary's. It would be a much easier move and from a personal standpoint, it made more sense than moving to Thomasville. "I guess so," she said. "I'm committed to doing the job, so I guess it doesn't matter where."

"Good. That's what I wanted to hear." Jack stood up, looking noticeably calmer. "I'm sorry about all the last minute scrambling this will mean, but you and Dillon will have to go to Weston and work on things."

Stacie nodded. "I guess we'll start by looking at the building and go from there."

"Then I'll leave it up to you to get in touch with Dillon and arrange things. I think you should do it as soon as possible, though. Next week maybe?"

"Of course."

"You're kidding! Weston?" Megan looked at Stacie incredulously and set her hamburger down on the plate in front of her. "That's so much closer to St. Mary's." Her delight was obvious. "For my own sake, I'm glad. It won't be so hard to see you."

Stacie turned the catsup bottle upside down and thumped the side of it; she had been meaning to buy a new one for at least two weeks but had not gotten around to it. "I'm glad about that part, too."

Megan's expression turned serious. "You don't sound excited."

Stacie did not answer; she just kept waiting for the catsup to crawl down the side of the bottle and onto her plate.

"What about Brad?" Megan prompted.

"What about him?" Stacie answered a little too abruptly.

"Well, if the whole reason you two broke up was because you had to move two hundred miles away, then maybe. . . ."

Stacie shook her head. "I don't know, Megan. Lately I've been thinking there had to be more to it than that."

"What do you mean? Brad would take you back in a second."

"Sure, now that he could have what he wanted all along. I don't want him to 'take me back,' Megan. I don't know how this change affects my relationship to Brad, but if we're going to get together, we'll have to have a better understanding about what we both want. Maybe we didn't know each other as well as we thought we did."

"Aw, come on, Stace." Megan crossed Stacie's small, tidy kitchen to get a napkin. "You two had a great relationship, and it doesn't have to be over. You can both have what you want this way. Brad works on jobs all over the county, so whether he lives here or in Weston won't matter."

"Can we change the subject, please?" Stacie bit into her hamburger and then said with her mouth full, "Are you going out to the Homestead tomorrow?" She knew Megan did not want to let go of talking about Brad, but Stacie just did not feel up to it. And she was not sure Megan would understand her confused feelings about Dillon, so she did not want to discuss him, either.

"No, I can't go tomorrow," Megan answered. "But some of the others are going. Brad is going, for instance."

"Megan!"

Stacie finally succeeded in getting Megan to talk about something else, but her own mind brimmed with the exact questions her friend had raised. *What did this change mean about her engagement to Brad? Should she tell him right away and expect to pick up where they left off? Should she wait until the move actually happened and see how he reacted?* It had been more than four months since the night they broke their engagement. Maybe they had drifted far enough apart in that time that they did not belong together anymore. And, although she knew she still had strong feelings for Brad, Stacie also felt a lively spark when she thought about Dillon. What did that mean?

"Thanks for meeting me here," Stacie said as she fumbled in her jacket pocket for her keys.

"No problem," Dillon answered. "Weston is so close to you that it makes sense to go together from here."

Stacie locked her apartment door and dropped her keys back into a pocket. "Then, let's get going."

The drive to Weston took just under an hour. This time it was Stacie who was familiar with the local area and could point out the interesting buildings and places shrouded in legend. When she pulled her car into the parking lot of the building they had come to see, she was impressed.

"From the outside, it looks like a great building," Stacie commented as she slammed the car door.

Dillon was scanning the neighborhood. "Great location. It will be easy for people to find, and it looks like it's right on the bus route."

"Let's check it out," she said.

They got out of the car and approached the front door of the building. Dillon produced a key Jack had gotten from the owner and turned it in the lock. They stepped inside to a room filled with daylight streaming through the large front windows. Despite this, Stacie remembered her cautious steps in the darkness of the Thomasville building and the way Dillon had confidently guided her across the room.

"Ah, this time the light switch is right next to the door," Dillon said, as if remembering the same moment. Although it was not really necessary, Dillon flipped the switch and fluorescent lights hanging from the ceiling started to hum and flickered on. It was obvious that the building had been an office complex. The large reception area with worn gray carpeting was the focal point for four modest offices. At the rear was a hallway leading to another large room, this one with exposed cement floors and utility shelving on the walls.

"Must have been a warehouse," Dillon speculated.

"We could section off a portion for a supply room and convert the rest to a place to eat," Stacie said, pacing the length of the room. "We could seat about sixty people in here, I would think."

Dillon was nodding. "Apparently there are more offices upstairs."

"Sleeping rooms."

"Right. But for how many beds?"

"Let's go up and take a look."

It took only a few more minutes for Dillon and Stacie to be satisfied that the building would be adequate.

"I think we can tell Jack that this will work out, if he can come to an agreement with the owner," Dillon said. "Now, all we need is a contractor."

Stacie resisted the urge to mention that she knew a contractor. "I guess we'll have to start all over again with getting bids."

"We've lost a lot of time, and it might be hard to find someone who will do indoor work during the good summer weather."

"If we can find a contractor, how soon can we open?"

Dillon tilted his head in thought. "Maybe by the fall. We'll have to see how much red tape the city will make us wade through."

"On to city hall, then."

After a quick lunch, they spent the rest of the day collecting the names of all the city officials they would have to contact and finding out what Weston's city council would need to know about their plan before approving it. Their vigorous conversation flowed with ideas, and Stacie filled page after page in her notebook.

It was almost supper time when they headed back to Stacie's car and started the drive back to St. Mary's. The hour passed quickly—too quickly. Even though it was work that brought them together, Stacie had thoroughly enjoyed the day with Dillon. She was invigorated by being with someone who shared her vision, and she especially appreciated Dillon's mild-mannered approach to getting things done. He did not get ruffled; he just kept working at one task after another until he was satisfied with their progress.

When they reached the city limits, Stacie toyed with the idea of asking Dillon to come to her apartment for dinner. Mentally, she inventoried her refrigerator to see if she had the fixings for a meal. She could offer something simple, like pasta and salad. But would she be crossing over an invisible line if she invited Dillon home to dinner? Their hours together had been filled only with business. Although Dillon was warm and congenial toward her, how could she know that he did not relate to everyone with that same warmth? She decided against asking him if he was free that evening and took the exit off the highway that would take them to his hotel.

She pulled into the parking lot and slowly maneuvered to the main entrance. "How's your room here?" she asked pleasantly.

"Not too bad. It could use a fresh coat of paint, but it's clean and quiet."

"It's an historic building, you know," Stacie pointed out knowledgeably.

Dillon smiled curiously. "I can tell by the plumbing."

Stacie burst out laughing and Dillon joined her.

"Have a nice evening, Stacie. I'll see you at the office in the morning."

Stacie did not immediately pull away from the curb; she watched, mesmerized, as Dillon pulled open the oversized door and was swallowed up by the mammoth building. She had a twinge of regret at not having invited him to dinner, but it was too late now.

Dillon was around the office most of the next day. There was no desk for him to use, so he sat at a small wooden table across from Marsha in the reception area. Stacie had offered to share her limited space, but Dillon insisted that he would be disturbing her too much and that he was getting along just fine at the table. Marsha scowled at him from time to time for tying up her phone, but Dillon just flashed his irresistible smile and gradually won her over. Before the day was out, Marsha was offering to help Dillon with his calls.

They had agreed the day before that Dillon would set up the appointments they needed and Stacie would work on pulling together a proposal for the city council. She could use the Thomasville proposal as a guide, but many of the details had to be changed. Fortunately, Dillon had put his original proposal on computer disk, so it was fairly easy to work on the revisions. By the end of the day, Stacie had a draft completed and a list of additional information about Weston she would need to have before she could finish the job.

She was packing up her briefcase, getting ready to go home, when Dillon knocked on her door frame. "I think we're all set for three appointments in Weston next week," he said.

"That's great."

"Took me all day to get that far; those city people don't want to be pinned down."

Stacie smiled. "The important thing is that you got the appointments."

"I suppose so."

"Will you be staying in St. Mary's until next week? Or are you going home and coming back again?

Dillon shrugged. "There's really nothing that I have to be

in Thomasville for. In fact, I should start looking for a place to live in Weston. Maybe I'll spend a few days doing that."

Stacie nodded at his sensible plan. "I'm sure Jack would like to have you around here for a while, too."

"I like hanging around here. I've finally got Marsha softened up. How tough can things be when I've accomplished that?"

They both laughed.

"Well, I see you've got your briefcase ready, so I guess you're on your way home," Dillon said. "You're not taking work home, are you?"

"Just a little," Stacie said apologetically, fingering the strap on her briefcase and looking away from Dillon. "Stuff to read mostly."

"I have a better idea."

Stacie glanced up. "What's that?"

"Let's have dinner together."

"Well, I. . . ." Inside, Stacie was leaping at the invitation. Outwardly, she did not want to misinterpret it.

"You've lived here for six years. Surely you know some good restaurants."

"As a matter of fact, I do," Stacie answered, more composed. "We've both been so busy today that we haven't had much chance to talk about how things went yesterday. Dinner would be a good chance to do that."

Dillon leaned against the door frame and smiled with one side of his mouth. "That wasn't exactly what I had in mind."

Stacie's heart was beating faster and she fumbled for words. She decided to change the subject. "Well, I'd like to go home and freshen up. Can I meet you somewhere in about an hour."

"I'll pick you up, and then you choose the restaurant."

Stacie nodded awkwardly. "Fine. Do you remember how to get to my apartment?"

"It isn't hard. I'll see you in an hour."

Three hours later Stacie and Dillon were walking up the sidewalk to her apartment building, acting out the best jokes they knew and laughing conspicuously. If neighbors looked with disfavor on the disruption of the quiet spring evening, they did not notice. Stuffed with Italian food, they were experimenting with Italian accents in their conversation and gesturing wildly as the owner of the restaurant had done all evening. When they got close to the building, Stacie put a finger to her mouth. "Shhh. We'd better quiet down. I've got some older neighbors who go to bed pretty early."

"I know it's a work night, Stacie, but I hate for this evening to end."

"I had a great time, Dillon. I haven't laughed that much in weeks." They were standing outside her door now. She reached into her pocket for her keys. "I should have left the porch light on. I can barely see the keyhole."

"I'm glad you left it off."

That strange remark caught Stacie's attention and she looked up at him.

Dillon put his fingers lightly on her chin. "I'm glad you left the light off because it makes it easier to do this." He bent his head to kiss her and Stacie forgot all about looking for her keys.

seven

"Stacie! I found them!" Margaret Barrows leaned precariously out the window of the dining hall and hollered in the direction of the shed.

Stacie popped her head out of the musty shed, wiped the stray copper lock of hair off her forehead, and squinted back at Mrs. Barrows. The older woman gestured for Stacie to return to the building which housed the somewhat dilapidated kitchen and rustic dining room.

"They were here all along," Mrs. Barrows said once Stacie was within easy hearing distance. "I can't imagine how we missed them the first time we looked." She held the door open for Stacie and pointed toward the kitchen.

Stacie, her hair braided down the back of her neck to keep it out of the way while she worked, went into the kitchen and stooped to look inside one of several cardboard boxes tucked away in a corner cupboard. There were all the plates, cups, and bowls which Mrs. Barrows had lost track of during the years the camp was idle. The beige plastic dishes were tightly stacked, but Stacie estimated that there were place settings for close to one hundred campers. "Do you think this is all of them?" she asked.

"Oh, I think so, yes, that looks right." Mrs. Barrows glanced at her wristwatch. "They'll all need to be washed, but let's take a break first. I made some lemonade this morning." She smiled affectionately at Stacie. "My dear, will you help me pour? It's quite warm today; I'm sure everyone will want some."

"Of course." Stacie brushed her hands together to loosen some of the dust and then followed her friend up the small hill to the cottage. As always, she was amazed at the vigor which the kind, gray-haired woman displayed. Margaret Barrows roamed the camp with the energy of someone half her age—or less—Stacie thought, especially when she was having trouble keeping up with her. More than once Stacie had been out of breath as she trailed behind Mrs. Barrows along the woodsy paths leading to the cabins and outbuildings dotting the landscape of the Homestead.

By the time they got to the cottage, Stacie was ready for some lemonade. They took two glass pitchers brimming with refreshment and a stack of clear plastic cups and went to the shaded redwood picnic table outside the back door.

"Would you do the honors?" Mrs. Barrows asked, nodding her head toward the huge gong hanging from its own stand out in the yard.

"With gusto!" Stacie took the oversized mallet from its hook and swung. The gong reverberated so loudly that it would be impossible for anyone at the camp not to hear it. Sure enough, in a few seconds, workers began to straggle out of the various buildings and amble toward the picnic table.

The mid-May weather was more like the end of June. Finally, the spring rains had ended, and the earth at the camp turned from mud to dirt. Only last weekend the group had come in jeans and sweatshirts; now, most of them were in shorts and tee shirts, with sweat beading on their foreheads. Lemonade poured steadily out of Stacie's pitcher; she hoped that there would be enough to go around.

"That looks good, Stace." It was Brad's turn to come to the table.

Stacie had a fleeting, irritated thought that Brad could just as well have gone to Margaret's end of the table. But she dutifully surrendered the last of the lemonade in her pitcher and smiled as pleasantly as she had to all the others.

"What are you and Mrs. B. up to today?" Brad seemed determined to make conversation. He propped himself casually against the end of the table.

"Washing dishes." Stacie's answer was blunt and she glanced around the yard distractedly.

"Washing dishes?"

"Yes. Hundreds of them."

"Oh, you mean the camp's dishes," said Brad. "I thought they were lost."

"We found them. Now we're going to wash them."

"I see." Brad tilted his head straight back and tossed the contents of his glass down his throat. He set the empty cup down on the table. "I'll see ya, Stace," his said, his tone noticeably muffled.

Stacie did not return his farewell. Glad he was gone, she turned her attention to collecting the glasses left abandoned on the picnic table. She stacked them, tucked them under one arm, and picked up the empty pitchers. She was ready to return everything to the kitchen and get back to work.

"I suppose you know that you were quite rude to Brad."

Mrs. Barrows's direct tone caught Stacie off guard. Like a scolded school girl, she could not even offer a defense. "Well, I, I. . . ."

"You were a snob." Margaret took the glass pitchers out of Stacie's arms, pivoted on her left heel, and went through the back door.

"Why does he always talk to me?" Stacie pleaded pitifully, following Mrs. Barrows and setting the glasses in the sink.

"It's a fair enough question, my dear, given your history with Brad, but you needn't whine when you ask it."

Stacie looked at Mrs. Barrows with wide eyes. Had she really been whining?

"Let's leave these until later and get back to work on that stack in the dining hall." Mrs. Barrows held the door open for Stacie. "But don't think that I'm going to forget what we were talking about."

In the dining hall kitchen, Stacie wordlessly plugged the sink, turned on the hot water, and squirted detergent into the running stream. As the deep porcelain basin filled with suds, she lifted the plates out of their boxes and stacked them within easy reach.

Mrs. Barrows slipped a faded, yellow gingham apron over her head and tied it in the back. From a drawer she produced a stack of flour-sack dish towels. "Now, what's going on, Stacie?"

Stacie wanted to tell Mrs. Barrows how confused she was, but she didn't know how to start. Distressed, she plunged her hands into the water and began wiping plates.

"Really, Stacie, I don't think you're being fair to Brad. He cares about you very deeply, I'm sure of it."

"Mrs. Barrows, he's the one who wanted to break our engagement."

"You know very well that he didn't do that lightly. So that's no reason to be dismissive when he speaks to you."

"I just wish he wouldn't talk to me at all. It would be so much easier." She handed Mrs. Barrows the first of the plates to be dried.

"Stacie, pardon me for being so abrupt about all this, but I don't think you're telling me everything there is to tell."

"What do you mean?" Stacie focused her eyes on the dusty dishes.

"You've been acting strangely for the last couple of weeks."

"What do you mean?" Stacie repeated.

Mrs. Barrows put down her dish towel and turned to face Stacie. "You don't have to talk to me if you don't want to, Stacie." Her tone softened. "But you know that I want to listen if you need to talk."

They resumed their task and worked in silence for several minutes. Finally, Stacie spoke. "I'm not moving to Thomasville, Mrs. Barrows."

"Now we're getting somewhere. I knew something had changed. What happened?"

Stacie shook her head in frustration. "The building contract didn't work out. So my boss and the board of directors decided to try another location."

"Well, are you going to tell me where?"

"Weston."

"Oh, Stacie—that's so near. Aren't you delighted?"

"I suppose I should be."

"But you're not."

Again Stacie shook her head. "I was sort of looking forward to a chance to start over in a new place without all the baggage I'm dragging around here."

"By 'baggage' I suppose you mean Brad," Mrs. Barrows said.

Stacie nodded. "Megan thinks this should solve all my problems with Brad. Weston is close enough that we could live either here or there and both do our jobs."

"So?" Mrs. Barrows carried a stack of dry dishes to the cupboard and set them in their place. "You don't agree, do you?"

"Megan's idea is too much like a fairy tale; it has such a happy ending."

"Why shouldn't you have a happy ending, Stacie, dear?"

"Well, I guess I'm not saying that I don't deserve a happy ending. But I'm not sure that getting back together with Brad is the right happy ending."

Mrs. Barrows pinched her eyebrows together. "I think I need a bit more explanation. You told me just a few weeks ago that you still love Brad. Have your feelings changed?"

"I'm not sure." Images of Dillon Graves and Weston and an Italian restaurant filled Stacie's mind. She brushed these thoughts away to try to concentrate on her discussion about Brad. "I've been thinking a lot these last few months. And it seems to me that maybe our relationship was not so strong as we thought it was. If we had really been committed to each other, wouldn't we have been able to work something out? Was calling off the wedding the only option we had?"

"Do you believe in the goodness of God?" Mrs. Barrows asked.

"What?" The question seemed to Stacie to come out of nowhere. "Of course I believe in the goodness of God."

"You've had a tough life, Stacie. Your father left when you were eight; you're mother died when you were nineteen. You worked hard against the odds, to get through college. And then Brad failed you."

A tear escaping from one eye, Stacie's hands fluttered uselessly in the dishwater.

"Stacie, dear, you do deserve something good. Maybe working in Weston so you and Brad can be together is something good that God wants to give you."

"But you don't understand, Mrs. Barrows. There's more

to it than that."

"If you want to tell me. . . ."

"I met somebody else. At least, I think I have."

Mrs. Barrows waited patiently for Stacie to continue.

"His name is Dillon, Dillon Graves, and he's going to be the director of the new shelter." She sighed deeply. "I'm not sure I understand what's happening between us, because it's been so fast. At first I thought I was imagining things; he's nice to everybody, not just me. But a couple of nights ago we went out to dinner, and we had a great time. It was obvious that his interest is not just professional." Stacie thought of his kiss outside her apartment—definitely not professional interest.

"And you share his 'interest?'" Mrs. Barrows prompted.

More composed, Stacie resumed her washing motion. "I'm not sure. I like him a lot, I feel very comfortable with him, and we have a lot in common. But I was with Brad for so long. I'm not sure how I feel about getting involved again."

Mrs. Barrows voice was soft. "Maybe that's because you are not yet uninvolved with Brad."

Stacie shifted her weight to look at her companion. "But it's been five months, Mrs. Barrows. It's over between us."

"I've heard you say that several times. Yet, you also say you love him."

"I do! That's why I'm so confused. I think I love Brad, but if I really do, why do I feel so attracted to Dillon?"

Mrs. Barrows slung her dish towel over her shoulder and reached out to hug Stacie from behind. "I can't answer all your questions, Stacie. But I can remind you of the goodness of God—and the love of God. And I can tell you again how close I came to marrying the wrong man. Oh, I suppose

I would have been happy with Henry, but it would never have been the same as it was with David."

"In any event," Stacie said with forced cheer, "my confused feelings are no excuse for being rude to Brad. It's handy to blame this mess on him, but it's not really his fault."

Mrs. Barrows gave Stacie's shoulder one last squeeze and grabbed a fresh dish towel. "When are you going to tell Brad about Weston?"

"Megan thinks I was crazy not to have called and told Brad everything the moment I found out."

"I think we've established that Megan is a romantic at heart. I want to know what you think."

"I'll have to tell him. I can't keep it a secret from everyone forever. Pretty soon everyone in the group will know and it wouldn't be fair for Brad to find out from the grapevine," Stacie said. "Have you got a spare minute, Mrs. Barrows?"

Stacie's heart nearly skipped a beat when she realized that she was not alone with Mrs. Barrows any longer. They had been so engrossed in their conversation that they had not even noticed the creak of the screen door when it opened or the slap that it usually made when it shut.

Even before she turned around, Stacie knew she would see Brad standing at the door.

"What do you need, Brad?" Mrs. Barrows said cheerfully.

"We'd like your opinion on a landscaping problem, if you don't mind."

"I'd be glad to come take a look, but I'm sure whatever you all decide would be perfectly fine." Mrs. Barrows wiped her hands dry and casually tossed the towel on the counter. "Where have you been working today?"

"Out behind the old barn. Some of the guys are worried about the slope back there. Does it get pretty muddy when it rains?"

"Yes, we have had a problem in the past. I'm not sure there's much that can be done about it. . . ." Their voices trailed away as they went out the door. This time Stacie did hear the harsh slap when Mrs. Barrows let go of the door; why hadn't Brad fixed that spring yet, she wondered.

The plates were clean and dry, but the bowls and cups were waiting. Stacie looked at the grayish-brown concoction in the sink and decided it was time for some fresh water. Blindly she reached through the dirty liquid and pulled the drain plug. At first she thought it was not going to drain, but finally she detected some reluctant circular motion in the water. When the basin was empty, she started the process all over again.

While she pushed herself through these motions, Stacie's heart was still in her throat. *How long had Brad been standing there? How much had he heard?* He had spoken only to Mrs. Barrows, without acknowledging Stacie's presence at all. Stacie thought that could have been because she had been so short with him during the lemonade break; but it also could have been because he had heard her talking about Dillon. In her anxiety, she was washing dishes rapidly and piling them high in the dish drain. Out of necessity, she stopped washing and started drying with the dish towel Mrs. Barrows had discarded on the counter. Now, she felt even more pressure to decide what to do about telling him the news concerning Weston. She had do something soon; but she simply was not ready to have an emotional encounter with Brad.

The door creaked and slammed, and Mrs. Barrows returned. "I see you got along well enough without me," she said crisply.

"I changed the water," Stacie replied matter-of-factly, without looking at Mrs. Barrows. "The sink didn't seem to be draining very well. Maybe you should have somebody take a look at it."

"I'll be sure to do that." Mrs. Barrows cautiously approached Stacie and stood next to her to resume drying the dishes. After a moment of awkward silence, she spoke. "I don't think he heard anything, Stacie, if that's what's bothering you."

Stacie laughed unexpectedly. "How do you always know what I'm thinking?"

Mrs. Barrows shrugged. "Perhaps because we are so much alike."

"He would never say anything, you know," Stacie said.

"I suppose not. So why not ignore the fact that he was here and continue with the plans you were making to tell him yourself?"

"I just don't want him to think my working in Weston instead of Thomasville will automatically change anything between us."

"Maybe it won't," Mrs. Barrows speculated, drying the last dish. "Then again, maybe it will. You will think about it, won't you?"

eight

Stacie looked at the clock again, the fourth time in the last ten minutes. It was eight minutes until the time the meeting was supposed to start, so she decided to make the coffee.

Megan had given her a coffee bean grinder last Christmas, and Stacie had taken up the pleasure of having gourmet coffee for special occasions, attributing this indulgence to the influence of the receptionist at work on Friday mornings. She took out a small bag of French-vanilla coffee beans, carefully measured enough for one pot of coffee, and dribbled them into the top of the grinder. Following the instructions precisely, she pushed the button and counted to thirty before releasing it. Satisfied that the beans were ground finely enough, she pulled a filter from the cupboard and finished getting the pot set up. Glancing at the clock yet another time, she went ahead and turned on the coffeepot.

While she waited for the coffee to brew, she reached up into the cupboard above the refrigerator and took down a small oak tray and some simple, white porcelain mugs. From the basket of napkins which always sat on her kitchen counter, she selected four, each bearing the message, "Welcome Friends," and placed them neatly between the mugs.

Stacie carried the whole tray out to the living room and set it down in the center of the coffee table. Although she had done it earlier, she could not resist the urge to punch up the throw pillows on the couch and straighten the stack of magazines on the end table. It was three minutes until starting time. Where was everyone?

As the coffee dripped steadily into the pot, Stacie wondered how she had gotten herself into this predicament in the first place. Weeks ago at church she had signed a sheet saying she was willing to work on a camp publicity committee, and somehow she found herself hosting a meeting with three other people, one of them being Brad. At least Jenna was not coming, Stacie thought with relief. The other two committee members, Donna and Paul, were creative people with lots of good ideas, in Stacie's opinion, and she expected to enjoy working with them. *But why was Brad involved? Wasn't it enough that he was in charge of the work out at the camp?*

Guilt overwhelmed Stacie for the umpteenth time. Despite her intentions and her promises to Mrs. Barrows, she still had not brought herself to apologize to Brad for her curt behavior, and she was certain that that would hang in the air between them tonight. But with Paul and Donna there, they would be forced to focus on the real reason for the meeting, which was not to resolve their personal problems but to plan a publicity strategy to find children who wanted to go to camp.

As she went to make sure the porch light was on, Stacie caught a glimpse of herself in the mirror next to the door. Her pink top made her cheeks look rosy and highlighted her blue eyes. Her full, coppery hair hung loose in a casual style well past her shoulders. She squinted into the mirror and wondered what she would look like if she were ever brave enough to cut her hair. She knew she was attractive, but she also thought her long, girlish hair made her look too young. Maybe she should look at some magazines, she decided, to see if she could find a hairstyle she liked.

The ringing phone jolted her out of this vain consideration; she crossed back to the kitchen, picked it up, and said hello.

"Hi, Stacie, it's me, Donna."

"Hi, Donna. Where are you?"

"I'm sorry to be calling at the last minute, but I'm not going to make it to the meeting tonight."

"Is everything okay?"

"Well, I had car trouble on the way home from work and finally had to have the car towed. I'm still at the garage. I called someone to come and get me, but I don't know when that will be. I hate to miss the first meeting, but. . . ."

"Don't worry about it," Stacie said, forcing herself to be lighthearted. "We'll just assign all the jobs to you. Isn't that what happens when you miss a meeting?"

What Stacie was really thinking about was that now there would be only one person, Paul, to act as a buffer between her and Brad for the rest of the evening. She really could sympathize with Donna's problem, however, and chastised herself for even allowing her thoughts to stray from Donna's very real circumstances to her own selfish concerns. "I'm sure we'll have other meetings," she said. "I'll let you know if we decide anything tonight."

She hung up the phone just as the doorbell rang. For some reason, she had imagined that Paul would arrive first, so, when she opened the door and saw Brad standing on the step, she was taken aback for a moment.

"Am I the first to arrive?" Brad asked.

"Yes, yes, you are." Suddenly Stacie realized she had positioned herself firmly in the doorway. Quickly she stepped aside. "Come on in and sit down." Stacie swallowed hard as she followed Brad into the living room. This was not going to be easy.

"I wonder where everyone is." Brad looked questioningly

at Stacie and sat down on the couch.

"Donna just called," she explained. "She can't make it. Car trouble."

"That's too bad." Brad shook his head. "She really needs a new car. I wish there were some way I could help her get a good deal on one."

"Anyway, that leaves you and me and Paul. He should be here any minute." Stacie felt awkward standing up, but she was not sure where to sit. If she sat on the couch next to Brad, that might make things worse. If she sat in the chair across from him, he would have more opportunity to give her that piercing look which always weakened her, and that would not be any good. Finally she decided not to sit at all.

"How about some coffee?" she offered.

"Great. It smells wonderful. French vanilla?"

Stacie nodded. "It should be just about ready. Excuse me."

As she grabbed the handle of the coffeepot and checked to be sure that no loose grounds had worked their way down into the coffee, she kept her eyes off of Brad. In selecting French vanilla, she had suppressed the knowledge that it was Brad's favorite; now she wished she had chosen anything else, even just normal coffee.

Back in the living room, she picked up a mug and filled it with steaming brown liquid. The light scent escaped the pot and perfumed the air pleasantly. She had to admit it did smell appealing. She set the pot down next to the mugs and compelled herself to sit down in the chair across from Brad.

Brad looked at the wall behind her. "That picture is new, isn't it? The one with the carousel?"

"Yes, it is." Stacie was glad for an impersonal topic of conversation. "I found a whole set of prints in a shop. I loved them all, but I had to be realistic; I could afford only one."

"Well, you chose well, I'm sure. The colors are perfect with the other things you have."

"Thank you." What else could she say? All of her furnishings, most of them acquired during their engagement, had definitely been influenced by his tastes. The colors, the styles, the assortment of things were all choices they had made together in expectation of furnishing a home of their own some day. When they broke up, she offered to give him whatever he wanted from the collection, but he had refused to take anything. This was the first time he had been at her apartment since that painful night.

She stood up. "I fixed some stuff to nibble on. Why don't I get it for you."

"Well, I had a big supper. . . ."

Already on her way to the kitchen, Stacie was not deterred. "I'll just set it out, and maybe we'll feel like having something after we get started."

"I wonder what's keeping Paul."

Yes, Stacie thought. Where are you, Paul? Please get here soon.

The tray she carried to the living room had three kinds of crackers and two kinds of cheese meticulously arranged in a circular pattern. She forced herself to smile as she set it down in front of him. "Maybe Paul will be hungry when he gets here."

The phone rang again, and Stacie's stomach instantly soured. Hesitantly, she picked up the receiver. It took only a moment to find out that her intuition was right; Paul was not coming, either. She was going to be alone with Brad.

"Paul?" Brad questioned.

Stacie nodded.

"Not coming?"

"Nope. Too tired. He's working twelve-hour shifts, six days a week."

"Plus helping out at the camp," Brad pointed out. "He hasn't missed a weekend since we started."

Stacie nodded her understanding of Paul's situation, but she did not know what to think about her own.

As if reading her thoughts, Brad stood up, "Well, I guess I could leave and we could try to set this up for another night."

To her own surprise, Stacie disagreed. "I don't think we should put it off any further. We're weeks behind already and we really should have started on publicity at the same time we started the refurbishing project."

Brad shrugged his shoulders. "I think you're probably right about that. I suppose I can stay, if you want to give it a try."

"I'm not sure if our ideas will be as good as the ones Donna and Paul have," Stacie said, "but I'm willing to work at it if you are."

Brad gestured toward the couch. "Let's get started, then."

Stacie picked up the clipboard she had gotten out in anticipation of this meeting and settled into one corner of the couch. With one foot tucked underneath her, she stuck the end of her pen between her teeth while she reflected for a moment. "Maybe we should start by making a list of all the ideas we have, and then go back through them and see which are the best."

"That sounds like a good plan." Brad leaned back comfortably. "Let's see, I think Pastor Banning has some children in mind from the neighborhood that he'd like to see go to the camp."

"Do you know who any of them are?"

"No, but we could get a list of names from him and then check with their parents."

Stacie dutifully made the first entry on her list.

"We could make up a bulletin insert," she suggested, "and distribute it to all the churches in town. A lot of church camps are filled up by now, so there may be some children who will be surprised to find out there's still a chance to go to camp this year."

"Good thinking."

"And I know a few children from the shelter downtown. If we could figure out a way to cover their costs, I'm sure they would love to go."

"I hate to see money be a problem for any child. We'll work on scholarships. Go ahead and write down their names," Brad said, pointing to her clipboard.

"What about newspaper ads?"

"That would be a good way to let the community know what's going on out at the camp," Brad agreed. "But it could be expensive. Will we be able to afford it with the budget we're working with?"

Stacie twitched her nose. "It would probably blow everything we have, which isn't very much."

"Well, write it down anyway, just in case."

As she wrote, Stacie gradually brightened. "Hey, what about the religion page?"

"What about it?" Brad tilted his head to listen.

"The paper runs a religion page every Saturday. We could ask the religion editor if he would be interested in a human interest story."

"Hey, I think you're on to something here." Brad, sitting

at the other end of the couch, twisted to face her.

"It would be completely free publicity. We've done stuff like this for the shelter. The paper could send out a reporter, or we could find someone to write the story, get a few good photos. . . ."

"They would have to agree it's a great story."

"And Mrs. Barrows is certainly an interesting human," Stacie observed.

"Quite so, my dear, quite so," Brad said.

Stacie laughed out loud at his perfect imitation. When she regained control, she said, "It would certainly be more worthwhile than some of the stuff that gets published in that paper."

"Absolutely. The editor will jump at it."

"Okay." Stacie turned back to her list. "Have we got any other ideas?"

"Let me see. . . ." Brad casually reached for a cracker and popped it in his mouth. "We could put posters in the store windows downtown."

"Or hand out flyers at the grocery store," Stacie added, also reaching for a cracker with a dab of cheddar cheese on it. She put her clipboard down on the couch and reached for the coffeepot.

Brad picked up the list and looked it over. "I think we've already got some good ideas here. Do you think Donna and Paul are still willing to help out, even though they couldn't come tonight?"

Stacie was quick to reassure him. "I'm sure they are. Well, realistically, Paul may not have much time to give, but I know Donna really wants to do this."

"She's pretty artsy. Maybe she could work on the things that need to be printed and we could do some of the other legwork."

Stacie craned her neck to check the list again herself. "I could call the newspaper and see if they're interested."

"And check on the children from your shelter."

"Right." She scooted toward the center of the couch and put her hand out for the clipboard. Brad moved it so she could see better, but he did not let go of it.

"So I should talk to Pastor Banning," he said, "and arrange to visit with the families of those children."

"You always do a good job with visiting people."

They sat side by side on the couch now, their shoulders rubbing lightly against each other and their heads nearly touching as they bent over the clipboard together. Absorbed in their planning, Stacie, surprisingly, had easily put aside her discomfort at being alone with Brad. After only a few minutes, several promising ideas had emerged. It crossed Stacie's mind that they would have to check with each other to see if they were really finding any campers, and she had some trepidation about continued contact with him. But, for the first time since their breakup, she felt comfortable in his presence. Maybe it would be possible for them to find a way to be friends.

Brad leaned back again, and his hairy, muscular forearm brushed against her elbow. She liked the way it felt—and then immediately berated herself for responding to such a casual sensation. The inconsistency between thinking about being friends and the urge to respond to an accidental touch was bewildering. Nonchalantly, she moved away from him and refilled her coffee mug.

Brad picked up a few more crackers with his fingertips. Stacie took a swallow of coffee and listened to the crunch of the defenseless wafers against his teeth.

"Well, I guess one of us has to get in touch with Donna and see if she would be interested in doing these flyers," said Brad.

Stacie nodded. "I promised I would let her know what we decided. I'll call her."

Instinctively, Stacie thought that now that their business was done, this lull in their conversation was probably a good time to tell Brad about the change in plans for the new shelter. If she could bring herself to do it now, she would not have to make a special point about it later when the news hit the church grapevine. But first she would have to apologize. She was not sure which option was more difficult.

"Well, I guess there's not much more to be done tonight," Brad said, stretching his arms and stifling a yawn.

"I'll bet you're tired." Stacie weakly stated the obvious. If Brad left now, her chance to do this casually would be gone. But could she keep him here until she mustered up the courage she needed?

"I guess I'll be going, Stace." Brad stood up.

"Brad, please sit down."

He looked at her questioningly, but he complied.

"I need to say a couple of things." All the words which she had rehearsed to herself disappeared. "I'm not sure where to start. Yes, I am. I have to start with apologizing for the way I've been treating you lately."

Brad listened without speaking.

"I mean, you've been trying to be nice to me, and I've been really mean. Like last weekend at the camp. Please forgive me."

His hand moved slowly across the couch cushion between them, and he wrapped his fingers lightly around hers.

"I . . . I understand what you've been feeling, Stace.

People are not always themselves when they're in pain."

Her mind told her to extract her hand from his, but she made no move to do so. "I was dreading having you here tonight, but it's worked out all right, don't you think?"

He smiled and nodded. "It's been fine." He paused long enough to catch her gaze directly. "I've missed this place. I've missed you, Stace."

She broke from his gaze and looked down at their joined hands. The enormous lump in her throat made it hard to talk. "I've missed you, too, Brad," she admitted in a fragile voice barely above a whisper.

Brad moved over next to her and wrapped her in his arms.

"Brad, please, there's more I need to say."

"Shhh. Something tells me we'll have plenty of time for talking. Let me just enjoy holding you for a few minutes."

Instinctively, she returned his embrace. Mentally, she did not want to, but her heart gave her no choice. He slipped his hand around the back of her neck, under her hair, and urged her to turn her face to him. When she did, her lips met his.

Stacie had no further thought of resisting and she returned his longing kiss with all the fervor of the kisses during their engagement. The hand behind her neck began to move through her hair, while the other caressed her shoulders. Her own arms were now locked around Brad's waist. It was all very familiar. Her mind ceased to fight with her heart as she moved her hands up his back.

The phone rang.

Until that moment, Stacie had not realized how fast her heart was beating. She drew back from Brad's kiss.

"Let your machine pick it up," he urged, not releasing his hold on her shoulder.

The phone rang a second time. The interruption had

brought Stacie to her senses, and she was grateful for the opportunity to disengage and regain her perspective.

"I'd better answer it," she insisted. "It could be Donna," she added, although she did not think it likely.

Brad let go and she got up and answered the phone on the third ring.

"Hello. . . . Oh, hi, Dillon. How are you?"

Stacie was mortified. Why had she let Dillon's name slip out of her mouth? She felt caught. She was going to have to be rude to either Brad or Dillon, and given what had just transpired, she was not ready for them to be aware of each other—not like this. She lowered her voice as much as possible and carried the phone around the corner into the kitchen.

"I just wanted to see how you're doing," Dillon was saying.

"I'm doing fine," she said, "just fine." If she told him anything different, this whole situation would explode in her face. "Actually, I'm in the middle of a meeting with the camp publicity committee." She tried to make her tone sound light and wished that there were some people noises in the background. "Maybe we could talk another time?"

Dillon agreed to call in a few days, and Stacie hung up the phone. Her heart was pounding and she steeled herself to return to the living room and face Brad. If only she had let him go when he said he wanted to. None of this mess would have happened.

"Hi," Brad said simply when she returned to the room.

She forced herself to smile. "Hi."

He did not say anything else, but she sensed he was expecting her to offer some explanation. "That was somebody from work."

He poked out his lower lip and shrugged one shoulder. "I

never heard you mention anyone named Dillon before. Somebody new?"

"Yes." She studied his face, trying to figure out just how much she would have to tell him. "Actually, he's the director of the new shelter. I'll be working for him pretty soon."

"Oh." The silence hung thickly between them. "Isn't it a bit strange for your boss to call you at home on a Friday night?"

Stacie racked her brain for a believable explanation which had some semblance of truth. She could not come up with one fast enough.

"You're involved with him, aren't you, Stacie."

Stacie sighed and looked away, not answering. How could she? She was not sure herself whether she was involved with Dillon.

"Stacie, how could you kiss me like that a few minutes ago?" Brad's face was pale and pained. "How could you let me hold you like that without letting me know about him?"

At last Stacie defended herself. "There really isn't anything to let you know about. We've been out a few times, that's all."

"What do you mean, 'out a few times?' "

"Why are you grilling me? Dillon is a friend." She started getting sarcastic. "I suppose you'd say the same thing about Jenna."

"Why are you bringing Jenna into this?"

"I saw the two of you at Katie's Kitchen that night. It looked to me like you were enjoying her company quite well."

"I only went out with Jenna because you didn't want me anymore."

Stacie could hardly hold back the torrent of tears. "I never said that! I never said I didn't want you. You're the one who broke our engagement, or don't you remember that detail? You wanted to call all the shots."

Brad was silent. She could see he had clamped his jaw shut to control his words. Why hadn't she done the same? Never during their entire relationship had they ever shouted at each other like this. How had they moved so quickly from their closeness on the couch to barking at each other across the room?

"Good night." Brad left, and Stacie let the tears flow.

She collapsed on the couch and hugged a throw pillow to her chest where only a few minutes ago she had held Brad. There was no question in her mind now that she still loved him, despite her confused feelings for Dillon. Poor Dillon was getting caught in the middle of something he did not know anything about.

Stacie reached up to click the lamp off and then picked up a box of tissues from the end table. Deep sobs welled up inside her, building up force until she was crying hysterically. Using one tissue after another, she blew her nose and wiped her eyes until she got herself under control, at least outwardly.

Inwardly, she could not have been more out of control. She thought about calling Megan, but she had never told Megan about Dillon. She could call Mrs. Barrows, but then she would have to admit she still had not told Brad about moving to Weston. The plain fact was that she was too exhausted to make explanations to anyone, so she suffered alone. When she was done crying, she pulled the afghan off the back of the couch and huddled in the dark.

The hours passed silently and painfully. Finally she slept, too spent even to fight the disturbing images of her dreams.

nine

Stacie was beginning to be annoyed by insistent thumping. Foggy from her fitful sleep, she was not sure where the noise was coming from, but she knew she did not like it.

There it was again, only louder this time and more like pounding. As her irritation rose, an excruciating pain pierced her left temple.

"Stacie! Are you in there?"

Sprawled on the couch, the afghan long ago fallen unnoticed to the floor, Stacie reluctantly opened her eyes at the urgent sound of Megan's voice. What was Megan doing here? What time was it? What day was it?

"Stacie, open this door right now or I'm going to call the police."

More banging. Stacie could hear Megan jiggling the doorknob. She almost believed Megan would call the police. Somehow she had to conquer the dry lump in her throat and make her voice work to let Megan know she was all right, at least physically.

"I'm coming," she croaked.

"Was that you, Stacie? You get over here and open this door."

Stacie pulled herself up on the couch and repeated, "I'm coming," this time a little louder. Leaning heavily on the coffee table, still strewn with last night's cold coffee, stale crackers, and dried cheese, she heaved herself up and lurched toward the door. She aimed at just enough furniture to support herself as she navigated across the room. With the door open, she held her hand to her aching head while Megan charged into the room.

"What took you so long to come to the door?" Megan demanded. "You had me worried sick that something terrible had happened to you." She paused and took stock of Stacie's unkempt and pained appearance. "Are you going to tell me what's going on?"

"Just let me sit down," Stacie groaned. "I've never had a hangover, but if it feels any worse than my head does today. . . ." Her voice trailed off, leaving the thought unfinished. She collapsed into the armchair and leaned her heavy head to one side, seeking support. "I'm always glad to see you, Megan, but what are you doing here?"

Megan's forehead scrunched up in a question. "It's Saturday."

That bit of information was not helpful to Stacie.

"The camp? Remember?" Megan prompted. "I came to pick you up so we could ride out together."

"Oh, yes. Saturday." Stacie's eyes were closed and it was hard for her to breathe. "Can you get me something for this headache?"

"Of course," Megan generously agreed. She shook a finger at Stacie. "But when I get back, I want to know why you have this headache and why you look like such a wreck."

Megan disappeared down the hall into the bathroom. Stacie could hear her rummaging around in the medicine cabinet, looking for some pain reliever, and then running water to fill a cup. In addition to the agonizing headache, Stacie's neck was strangely stiff from sleeping in an awkward position on the couch. Wincing with pain, she turned her head from side to side. Then, with extreme effort, she lunged from the chair back to the couch so she could be prone again.

Her mission accomplished, Megan returned with two white tablets and a small cup of water. Stacie propped herself up on one elbow just long enough to swallow the pills. She handed the empty cup back to Megan. "Thanks. I hope that helps."

"You look like you collided with a train, Stacie." Apparently Megan was not in the mood for an indirect route to the information she wanted. She propped herself on the edge of the coffee table, pushing away last night's tray. "Just exactly what went on here last night?"

Stacie pushed her hair back off her face, not sure what to say to her blunt friend.

"Does this have anything to do with Brad?" Megan probed suspiciously.

"It has everything to do with Brad," Stacie admitted. "We had a terrible fight."

"I thought you weren't even speaking to him. How could you have a fight?"

"We managed somehow."

Megan picked up the cold coffeepot. "I'm going to make some fresh coffee while you pull yourself together," she said in her sternest tone. "I want the whole truth and nothing but the truth."

Stacie nodded. "Coffee would be good."

While Megan clanked around in the kitchen making a fresh pot of coffee, Stacie tried once again to sit up, this time with more success. The horror of the night before was still fresh, but she was reconciled to the reality of a new day. At the very least she had to sit up.

Megan returned with a glass of orange juice in her hand. "I thought this would get you going while we wait for the coffee."

"Thanks." Stacie took a long, welcome sip, and the lump in

her throat diminished slightly. "Don't look at me that way, Megan. I will tell you what happened. Just give me a chance."

Megan kept silent, but her impatience was evident. Finally, Stacie started to talk. "Brad was the only one who showed up for the meeting last night. It was awkward, but we got through it. We even had a few good ideas. But then. . . ."

"Then what?"

Stacie looked away. "We started kissing."

"That's good, isn't it?" Megan said hopefully, trying to catch Stacie's eye.

Stacie studied her orange juice. "I'm not sure it was very smart, but I couldn't help it. It was too much like the old days when he was here so much."

"So how did kissing turn into fighting?"

"Is the coffee ready?" Stacie glanced toward the kitchen. She wanted coffee, but more than that she wanted time to figure what to say to Megan about Dillon. She had talked about Dillon in a general way, but never so that Megan would think there was any attraction between them. Now she would have to admit the truth.

Megan handed Stacie a mug of steaming coffee. "Well?"

"Well . . . the phone rang, and it was Dillon."

"So?"

"So, I haven't told you everything about Dillon. It wasn't a business call. We've been out together a couple of times."

"I see." Megan's jaw was firmly set. She reached up and nervously tucked her brownish hair behind one ear. Her gaze did not leave Stacie's face.

"I'm sorry I didn't tell you sooner, but there really wasn't anything to tell. We enjoy each other's company, but I'm not sure if it means anything."

"Apparently Brad thought it meant something, right?"

Megan knew Brad almost as well as Stacie did, so it was no surprise that she could predict his response.

Stacie nodded. "Right. He gave me the third degree, and I lashed back about seeing him with Jenna that night. You can fill in the rest."

Megan leaned back on the couch, cradling her mug. "Did you get any sleep at all?"

"Some. But I don't know if I'm up to going out to the camp today."

"I understand. Mrs. Barrows will understand, too."

Stacie shook her head. "No, Mrs. Barrows will have a thousand questions that I'll have to answer eventually, just like you did."

Megan smiled at the comparison. "We're good for you, Stacie. You know that. Otherwise you would just shrivel up and never talk to anyone."

"You're probably right about that." She set her mug down on the table. "Maybe if I take a shower, I'll feel better."

"You don't have to go today, Stacie. Brad will probably be there."

"At the moment, I don't even care. Besides, he was so mad last night, I doubt he would come anywhere near me today." She turned to look at Megan. "Will you wait for me?"

Trying vainly to control her wild hair, Stacie shuffled off to the bathroom and turned on the shower. When ready, she stepped gratefully into the steaming spray. The moist heat was therapeutic for her stiff neck and, in a few moments, she felt much better physically. Her emotional numbness persisted, but at least she was moving around more normally.

By the time she had finished showering and put on fresh clothes, she detected the smell of bacon and eggs coming from the kitchen. Megan was hard at work putting breakfast on the table. She looked up from setting the plates out and greeted Stacie as she entered the room. "Hi."

"What's all this?"

"No point in going out to the camp without eating. We're getting such a late start, we'll probably miss lunch."

"Sorry about that," Stacie said sheepishly. "I didn't know I even had any bacon."

"Well, you did, and it wasn't green or moving, so I used it. So here's breakfast. Eat." Megan scratched Stacie's back affectionately and smiled. "Remember when we were in college and I broke up with Doug?"

Stacie laughed. "Now there was someone who looked like she had collided with a train."

Megan agreed. "Yep. You took such good care of me. I thought there was never going to be any life after Doug, but you pulled me through."

"Aw, you're like a cat. You always land on your feet. Not like me; I roll over and play dead."

"Well, not this time. Not if Mrs. Barrows and I have anything to say about it." She gestured toward the table. "Let's eat while everything is hot."

The eggs were cooked over-easy, just the way Stacie liked them, although she knew Megan would have preferred scrambled eggs. The whole wheat toast already was spread with butter and orange marmalade, and the bacon was fried to a perfect crispness. Megan kept Stacie's juice glass filled throughout the meal.

They abandoned their earlier conversation and instead reminisced lightheartedly about Doug and other college friendships. They lingered over their empty plates for long after the time they should have been in the car and on the road. Normally it would have been easy for Stacie to feel guilt-ridden about her failure to be at the camp first thing in the morning, but Megan had a way of giving her unspoken permission to indulge herself in little pleasures. When she finally did carry her dishes to the sink, she took the opportunity to pour herself another cup of coffee, glad that it was just plain coffee—no gourmet flavored beans, especially no French vanilla, just plain, grocery-store coffee. It would be a long time before she would want any more French vanilla coffee. Maybe she would even give the bag of beans to Marsha at the office.

Megan insisted on washing the dishes, giving Stacie a few cherished minutes to sit quietly and alone in the living room. Looking around at her familiar things in this comfortable setting, she had an urge to start packing right away. She would not move to Weston for several more weeks, but a flash of insight told her that she should get out of this apartment where she had spent so much time with Brad. Maybe in a new city, in a new apartment, she would get him out of her system once and for all. Maybe she would even give away some of the things they had selected together and really start fresh. Perhaps then she could be sure she would never give in to him the way she had last night, knowing that the bigger question between them had not been resolved.

Despite her resolve to stay awake, Stacie dozed off during most of the forty minutes it took to drive to the camp. The indulgent morning with her best friend had purged her of the emotional tangle of the night before, and she was relaxed, even carelessly limp. Her half-dream state brought her images not of Brad or Dillon but of the caring hands of Megan pouring juice and turning eggs, and of Mrs. Barrows with her comforting trademark pot of tea. Only when the car came to a stop and Megan turned off the engine did Stacie revive and look around. "We're here already? Did you take a shortcut I don't know about?"

Megan flashed a broad false smile. "Don't try to be cute, you lazy bum. Nap time is over; we're here to work."

"Absolutely. I'm ready to roll up my sleeves and dig in."

They got out of the car and proudly surveyed the progress that had been made in recent weeks. The lush green lawn was neatly trimmed; bark chips layered two inches deep kept the weeds under control around the edges of the parking lot. The shed had been scrubbed and painted with a sturdy outdoor finish, and the rustic pine of the dining hall gleamed through its large windows. The narrow circular road leading to the cabins was clear of debris, and freshly-painted markers pointed to the various trails.

Stacie turned to Megan with satisfaction. "This place is really shaping up."

"Sure is. It looks even better now than I remember it as a child."

"I've lost track of what we're supposed to do today," said Stacie.

"Well, I think the insides of the cabins are ready for painting. But since we're so late, maybe we'd better check in with Mrs. Barrows."

Together they started for the cottage, hoping to find Mrs. Barrows there. They were almost to the door when they had to stop abruptly—Brad had appeared from around the back of the house and stood directly in their path.

"Good morning, Brad," Megan said with an even, cheerful tone.

"How ya doin', Megan?"

"Pretty good. What's going on here today?"

"A lot of painting." Brad spoke to Megan but looked at Stacie. "If you're looking for Mrs. Barrows, she's up in the first girls' cabin."

"Great. Maybe we can help up there," Megan answered.

Now Brad spoke to Stacie, oblivious to Megan's presence. "Can we talk for a few minutes, Stace?"

The question was simple and reasonable. Even a few days ago, Stacie would not have wanted to have a private conversation with Brad. Now she thought she really had nothing to lose. Brad had spoken only a few words, but they were enough to let her know that the anger of last night had dissipated for him as it had for her. The emotional calm that she had achieved during her pampered morning was unruffled, and she agreed to his request.

Megan excused herself gracefully and walked up the road toward the cabins, leaving Stacie and Brad standing alone outside the cottage.

"Maybe we could walk for a bit," Brad offered, gesturing toward a trail. "Have you been on the path to the duck pond?"

Stacie shook her head. "No, but I'd like to see it."

They sauntered in silence for quite a while. The spring foliage, fuller and greener than even a few days ago, proliferated along the path. Sunlight filtered through the leaves and left delightful patterns of shadows and light. Chipmunks, tiny and quick, darted between the trees faster than Stacie could turn her head to watch them. The path was level for the most part and quite easy to hike. Stacie had never been this far in; the wet spring had made the trails so muddy that it had not been very appealing to explore them. Today, with a foretaste of summer, the path boasted its best flora and fauna. Even though she was with Brad and could easily have felt awkward, the shared silence let her soak up every detail of the walk.

After about a mile and a half, they came to the duck pond. The swampy patch of land, too wet to walk across, was just barely too large to walk around. According to camp legend, occasionally there were ducks there; Megan said she had seen some one summer years ago. Today there were none, but Stacie did not really mind.

"There's a good sitting log right over there." Brad's observation was the first interruption to the silence of the last thirty minutes.

"Thanks. I'd like to sit and look around," Stacie said. "It's really beautiful here. I was wishing we had brought some bread crumbs along, but since there don't seem to be any ducks, I guess it doesn't really matter. I wonder how complicated it would be to get some ducks and bring them here before camp starts." Stacie realized that she was prattling but could not seem to stop herself. She knew Brad had not brought her up here to talk about ducks, but, sitting next to him on the log, she was suddenly nervous.

"Stacie, I want to apologize for last night."

She had not expected that. She picked up a stick and began scratching in the dirt without saying anything.

"I had no business raking you over the coals about having a boyfriend. It's just that I never expected you to be interested in somebody else so soon."

"Well, I. . . ." Stacie felt she should say something, but she was not sure what.

"Let me finish," Brad persisted gently. "It's just that I'm still insanely jealous, I guess. I love you, Stacie. It's hard to think about you with another guy. Now I know you think I've moved on because you saw me with Jenna. I want to explain about that, too."

"Brad, I'm sorry I threw that in your face. You don't owe me an explanation." She really did not want to hear about his relationship with Jenna, any more than she wanted to discuss her friendship with Dillon.

"But I want to explain," he insisted. "I went out with Jenna because she kept asking me out. As soon as she found out that we had broken up, she swooped in and circled around me. I tried to care about Jenna, but it just didn't work." Brad shifted his weight to turn toward Stacie, who was still scratching in the dirt. "Stacie, honey, Jenna doesn't hold a candle to you. I love you. I know you don't want me to say that, but I have to. I don't want you to think that I could leave someone like you and take up with Jenna McLean."

"I don't know Jenna very well, but she seems very nice."

"Oh, sure, she's nice. But she's not you." He put his hand on her forearm to stop her nervous action.

"Brad, please," she said, pulling her arm away but not looking at him. "Let's be careful. Last night things got out of control, and I don't just mean our tempers."

Brad shook his head. "I don't think so. I think what happened between us meant something to both of us. If I could get you to look at me, I would dare you to deny that."

Stacie said nothing. She couldn't deny it, and Brad knew it. It would be an outright lie to look him in the face and say that feeling his arms around her and returning his kiss had meant nothing to her. Although skittish at first, her response had been genuine and without regret—until the phone rang. *What turning point would they have come to if the phone had not rung? Or if it had been anybody other than Dillon?*

Not answering Brad would leave him with only one conclusion: that she agreed with him. She did nothing to dissuade him. When he leaned over to kiss her, she did not resist. While she did not respond with the abandonment of the night before, clearly she was responding, so he moved closer and wrapped his arms around her.

This time, although craving the moment, Stacie kept her head. She broke off the kiss and pulled away. "Let's take it easy, Brad. We're on rocky ground, and I don't know if we should be doing this."

"I love you, Stacie."

She looked him squarely in the eyes. "I know, but that doesn't mean everything is okay between us. We can't just pick up where we left off as if the last five months never happened."

It was Brad's turn to sigh and look away. "We'll work on it, Stace. Somehow we'll work it out."

Was this the moment to tell him that she only had to move to Weston, not Thomasville? Or would that seem like a quick fix to a bigger problem? She decided she would tell him. Even if she harbored fears about resuming their relationship, Brad was entitled to know. But how should she start? She could not just blurt it out.

While she struggled for the words, Brad interpreted her silence in his own way. "Well, I guess we should head back." He stood up. "The guys will be wondering where I am."

The moment was gone. Stacie comforted herself with the thought that at least they were on speaking terms. There would be another opportunity to tell him about Weston, perhaps when she was more sure of where their relationship stood.

Brad offered his hand and she accepted it to pull herself up off the log. But he did not let go of it, and she did not object. Once again they walked the trail in silence. She stopped several times along the way to gather a bouquet of wildflowers; each time Brad offered his hand again, and each time she accepted it.

When they came to the clearing where the cottage and dining hall stood, Mrs. Barrows was there. As soon as Stacie saw her, she gently but quickly dropped Brad's hand and used both of hers to hold the wildflowers.

"There you two are," Margaret Barrows said in a playfully scolding tone. "All this work to be done around here, and the two of you are off picking wildflowers."

Stacie smiled. "I'm sorry I didn't come this morning, but the day is not over. I am fully at your disposal for the rest of the afternoon."

Mrs. Barrows continued her scolding. "It's practically time to start fixing supper. Those flowers had better be for me."

Stacie laughed and held them out. "There is no one else so deserving."

"Since I have no peace offering, I'd better get back to work," Brad said sheepishly, glancing up the road toward the cabins. "I wonder if they need more paint up there." He headed off to the shed to gather his supplies.

"Well," Mrs. Barrows said, "you have quite a selection of flowers here. Let's get them into some water, shall we?" When she looked at Stacie, her eyes were full of questions.

But Stacie was not ready to talk. She was pondering this new plane in her relationship with Brad and trying to decipher what it might mean for the future.

"Enjoy the flowers, Mrs. Barrows," she said cheerfully. "I think I'll go see what Megan's up to."

ten

The pages of the worn brown hymnal rustled as Stacie found number 367 and stood with the congregation for the last hymn. When the organ introduction ended, she opened her mouth and sang with gusto.

By the time she arrived at the church this morning, the pew where Megan sat was too full to accommodate another person, so Stacie had taken a seat near the back with the other latecomers. She often sat near the front with Megan, especially since breaking up with Brad, because she disliked sitting alone. But, actually, she preferred sitting toward the back where she could survey the whole congregation: the graying heads of the pillars of the church; the squirming children anxious to escape; her friends from the college and career Bible study. For over five years she had been coming to this church every Sunday and Thursday. Ironically, she was the one who had first brought Brad to this church where he had quickly become a leader.

If she moved to Weston, it would be a long drive to come back here every week, but she hoped to stay in touch with the people. What kind of church would she find in Weston, she wondered. Did Dillon even go to church? They had never talked about it. When she was with Brad, it was easy enough to convince herself that her attraction to Dillon was merely an infatuation; but would she feel that way when she moved to Weston and worked with him every day? She chastised herself for letting her thoughts wander to Dillon.

The organ shifted into somber concluding tones and the

congregation sang a muted "Amen." With a twinge of guilt, Stacie realized she had not absorbed a single word of the hymn she had just sung. Actually, her mind had wandered more than usual during the entire service. She had taken notes on the sermon to force herself to pay attention, but even then she had lost the thread of logic somewhere after point two. Now she squeezed her eyes shut and focused on the prayer and benediction intoned by Pastor Banning. And then the organ brightened up and burst into a triumphant exit march.

The 263 people attending church that morning flowed into the aisles and moved slowly en masse out to the narthex. If Stacie had moved a little more quickly, she easily could have been out the door and into the sunshine, ahead of the crowd. But she was in no particular hurry, so she sauntered along listening to snippets of pleasant, Sunday-after-church conversations and returning the greetings of the people around her. Before long, she was happily trapped in the center aisle among the throng waiting to shake the pastor's hand. When she spotted Donna clear across the sanctuary in a side aisle, she remembered the publicity meeting. In all the emotional upheaval of the weekend, Stacie had forgotten about her assigned tasks. Donna was edging her way past people in a hurried way and would be gone long before Stacie could escape the crowd, so she settled for making a mental note to call Donna before the day was over. She had no plans for the afternoon; surely she would find a moment to do it.

"He's not here."

Stacie recognized Megan's voice, even in a whisper behind her, and turned around to greet her friend. "Who's not here?" Stacie asked in a full voice.

"You know very well whom I'm talking about," Megan persisted in whispering. "Where is he?"

Stacie shrugged. "How should I know? I hadn't even noticed he was missing."

"So you're going to play dumb, heh? I'll drag it out of you."

"Drag what out of me?" Stacie said with dry amusement.

"Everything." Megan widened her eyes dramatically. "I want to hear everything. You thought you were off the hook because Julie rode home with us last night, but today we will be all alone."

"What are you talking about?" Stacie laughed, moving a few steps up the aisle. "Did we have plans that I forgot about?"

"We have plans you never knew about," Megan corrected. "It's all been decided, so don't argue with me."

"I wouldn't dream of it," Stacie said with mock fear. "But would it be too much to ask exactly what has been decided?"

"We're going on a picnic, the first of the season," Megan informed her. "I have a cooler packed in the trunk of my car with everything we need." She gripped Stacie's elbow playfully. "So don't try to escape.

"Is this an elegant tablecloth-and-crystal picnic, or will I be allowed to change my clothes?"

"Well, if you promise to hurry," Megan reluctantly conceded.

They reached the end of the aisle. Without really stopping, Stacie absently extended her arm to shake the pastor's hand. He held onto her hand to get her attention.

"I wonder how the publicity meeting went the other night," he said. "Is there anything I can do to help?"

"Thanks for asking," Stacie answered. "Actually, Brad is supposed to get in touch with you for some names."

"I don't see him here this morning," the pastor said scanning the crowd.

Stacie was glad he did not ask her where Brad was; she really did not know. The fact was that she was curious herself, although she was reluctant to admit it. "I'm sure he will follow through, probably in the next couple of days."

Not wanting to hold up the exit line any longer, nor talk further about Brad, Stacie smiled graciously and stepped aside; Megan was not far behind.

"March straight out to the car, young lady," Megan commanded. "Let's not waste a moment of this glorious afternoon sunshine.

The end of May was turning out to be unbelievably like summer. Knowing that midwest weather could change in the space of a few hours, people all over St. Mary's were taking advantage of every gorgeous moment of the day. Swings filled with children squealing delightedly as they soared high above the sandpits, and the slides were slick from steady use. Softball fields were full of makeshift teams, and kites sailed through the air in scattered open fields. In neighborhood backyards, winter-white legs extended on chaise lounges in eager anticipation of the sun's rays. Three-year-olds determinedly peddled tricycles on the sidewalks, while six-year-olds tenaciously balanced atop two-wheelers.

Megan steered through the residential streets and out to the main highway, then picked up speed. They both rolled their windows down and let the wind whip through their long, loose hair.

"Where are we going?" Stacie howled above the gushing wind. The wind and sun felt wonderful, but it was nearly impossible to converse in the moving car.

"You'll know when we get there!" Megan called back. "I promise you'll like it."

"I hope you brought a lot of food. I'm ravenously hungry."

"All your favorites, I assure you."

Stacie turned her eyes back to the scenery outside her window. The trimmed lawns of the town gave way to split log fences around farm acreage laden with promising summer crops. Scattered tender green sprouts stood in bold relief to the black earth which nurtured them. The sky above them was a shining blue and boasted high, luminous, white clouds. Brown cows with random blotches of white sedately swung their tails at the swarming flies and chewed cud with an unbelievably slow but steady rhythm. Shirtless, a farmer sat high atop his tractor tilling a fallow field.

Spontaneously Megan broke out into an old camp song and, laughing, Stacie enthusiastically joined in. Songs they had not sung in ten years rang through the air. They could barely hear themselves above the roar of the wind, but they kept singing. When they had exhausted their supply of camp songs, Megan started in on her repertoire of kindergarten songs, and Stacie laughed even harder as she did the motions to *The Eentsy, Weentsy Spider* and *I'm a Little Teapot*.

Stacie gave herself fully to the release and exhilaration that such silliness brought. Twice in the last two days she had given in to kissing Brad—and enjoyed it, wanted it—and twice she had regretted it. She had known all along that they still loved each other, so really nothing had been resolved. The only change was that she had somehow gotten past wishing Brad would go away and leave her alone. She would not have to be rude to him in order to protect her wounded feelings from further attack. For weeks, even months, she had been in a complete funk because of their broken engagement. But she had come out of that dark tunnel now. She did not know what the future held for them, but she was ready to stop being a wounded wimp and take control of her life once again. And singing silly songs was helping.

She grinned at Megan at the end of the second round of *Twinkle, Twinkle, Little Star,* completely relaxed. Undoubtedly, Megan had brought her out here to get her to open up and talk, and she would oblige her soon enough. For the moment, it was enough just to be together with no sense of responsibility or time constraints.

Megan followed the car and made a left turn into a state park.

"I haven't been out here in ages," Stacie said with enthusiasm. "I wonder if the wildflowers are blooming on the hillside yet."

"That's exactly what we're here to find out." Megan passed the arrows pointing to the hiking trails and the picnic area and continued down the road she knew would take them deep inside the park where not many people bothered to go. Finally they parked the car and started walking up the hill on a narrow footpath, Megan's cooler suspended between them. They both knew where to go. They had come to a spot which had been a favorite during college, a place where they came when they wanted to be alone. All along Stacie had suspected this was their destination, and now she was delighted to be right.

Megan was well prepared. She had even brought the

proverbial red and white checkered tablecloth, which she spread on the ground at the top of the hill. Stacie sat down, waiting to be further pampered.

Megan reached into the cooler and pulled out a plastic container. "Chicken pasta salad," she announced, and reached in again. "Watermelon. Iced tea, lemon only. And of course, chocolate chip cookies."

"A perfect menu," Stacie said, reaching for the plastic picnic plates. I couldn't have done better myself."

Megan confessed that the chicken pasta salad was a new recipe, so they analyzed it as they ate. The watermelon provided ample seeds for a vigorous spitting contest, and the cookies were gooey and soft, just the way Stacie loved them. Satiated, they stretched out on the tablecloth and lay flat on their backs.

"This was a great idea, Megan," Stacie said with gratitude. "You can kidnap me anytime if we can come here."

"Well, you've been under so much stress the last few weeks. I figured you could use a little diversion."

"Mmmm." Stacie had her eyes closed contentedly. "Megan, tell me the truth. Do I bring all this on myself?"

"Define 'all this,' please."

"You know what I mean. You think I should just tell Brad about Weston and then marry him and live happily ever after. Do you think I make myself miserable because I don't take the easy way out?"

"Don't you want to marry Brad and live happily ever after?"

"I always thought I did." Stacie rolled her head and looked at Megan, who was staring up at the clouds. "But suppose I did marry him. What about the next time something like this happens? Will we be able to resolve it any better than we did this time?"

"You guys had a great relationship, Stace." Megan said emphatically. "I think you gave up too soon. Look what happened. If you had gone ahead with the wedding, you still would have found out you were moving only to Weston and everything would have worked out."

"It seems so simple when you say it." Stacie propped herself up on one elbow. "Why isn't it so clear to me?"

Megan shrugged one shoulder. "Maybe you're too hurt still. Brad let you down in a big way when he made you choose between the job and him. Maybe you don't trust him anymore."

"You're so wise, Megan," Stacie said, twiddling a blade of grass between her thumb and forefinger. "I do feel that way. But I also feel guilty."

"Why?" Megan's wide eyes looked at Stacie.

"Because I hurt Brad by the choice I made. Supposedly I loved him. How could I not choose to be with him?"

"As I recall," Megan said dryly, "God had something to do with your decision."

Stacie nodded. "At the time I really believed that, and I guess I still do." She flopped back down on her back. "So why would God make me choose between the job and Brad?"

"These are deep questions, my friend," Megan answered. "But I'm not so sure God is asking you to choose anymore."

Stacie did not respond. She lay still and felt the warmth of the sun through her eyelids. The soft earth beneath her conformed to her body, and the thick pad of grass cradled her form. She could not have been more comfortable home in her own bed. In the air was the exhilarating fragrance of spring. The wildflowers they had come to see dotted the meadow below them and perfumed the hillside and the very atmosphere around them shouted that winter was over.

More than anything, Stacie wanted to know that her own winter was over. It was possible now to be in Brad's presence and not be consumed with the hurt and guilt which had wracked her spirit during the spring months. Her downward, inward spiral had led to nothing but aggravation and, in that darkness, Dillon had been a luminous beacon. Dillon, knowing nothing of her past, beckoned her into the future. He would never be Brad, but could she be happy with him? She thought of Dillon's pleasant face and gentle demeanor and concluded yes, he was a fine man and they could have a promising future if she gave him the right signals. So why had she been kissing Brad during the last two days? She kissed him because she loved him, undeniably and passionately. But her questions about the strength of their relationship were deep; she was serious when she asked Megan what would happen the next time a similar problem came up. Blind love does not solve everything; life is not a fairy tale.

She sighed and readjusted her position. Glancing over at Megan, she decided her friend had dozed off. Stacie was physically relaxed, but her mind was racing too fast to sleep. She sat up and rummaged in the cooler for another chocolate chip cookie.

"I know exactly how many cookies are left, so don't think you can pull anything over my eyes."

Stacie laughed at the sound of Megan's voice.

"I thought you were sleeping."

"Maybe I was. But I know the sound of a chocolate chip cookie hunt when I hear it."

Stacie handed a cookie to Megan. "There are only four

left. We might as well finish them off."

Megan took a bite and chewed. "When was the last time you looked at the clouds, Stace?"

"What do you mean?"

"Look up there. The clouds are so puffy and white today. When was the last time you saw shapes in the clouds?"

Stacie shook her head. "Not for a long time." She settled back and looked up. "I used to lie in the backyard with my mother and tell stories about the clouds when I was little."

"Tell me what you see today."

"Come on, Megan. I just see clouds."

"Look again. Don't stop with the obvious." She pointed straight up. "See that one? It's a charging unicorn."

Stacie squinted at the bright sky. "I guess if you use your imagination, it could be a unicorn."

"Don't be such a fuddy duddy. Why do you think God gave you an imagination in the first place?"

"All right. I'll try." She surveyed the sky and selected a cloud. "That one over there is a doll house with a pointed roof."

"I can see that," Megan encouraged. "Try another."

For a long time they lay side by side on the checkered tablecloth picking out images in the sky. After a while they launched into adventurous stories about their imaginary characters. Megan's stories always had a happy ending; Stacie's stories always had a complication.

They lapsed into a contented, companionable silence. The afternoon was waning, but they had an unspoken agreement that they were not ready to go home.

"You know," said Megan lazily, "Mrs. Barrows usually has tea about this time of day."

One corner of Stacie's mouth turned up slightly. "Yes, it is about teatime, isn't it."

"We came pretty far south on the main road. If we just cut over to the east, we could be there in twenty minutes."

"But she won't be expecting us," Stacie protested.

"Can you honestly say you think that would matter to her?"

Twenty minutes later, they pulled up in front of Mrs. Barrows' cottage at the Homestead. With girlish giggles, they got out of the car and knocked on the front door.

Mrs. Barrows opened the door. "Why, Stacie and Megan, what on earth are you girls doing out here on a Sunday."

Stacie and Megan looked at each other and grinned secretly. "We were in the neighborhood, so. . . ." Megan said.

Margaret Barrows waved her hand in the air. "Nonsense. There is no neighborhood around here, and I don't work on Sundays. You came specially to see me. Well, I'm delighted. Please do come in. We must have tea." She ushered them into the living room. "I don't know what you two have been up to, Stacie, but perhaps you'd like a napkin to wipe that bit of chocolate out of the corner of your mouth."

Stacie's fingertip flew to her mouth and immediately detected the telltale evidence of her indulgence. Laughing, she explained, "We were having a picnic. Megan kidnapped me."

"And brought you here as a hostage?" Mrs. Barrows questioned.

Stacie shook her head emphatically. "No one would have to hold me hostage to get me to come here. I hope you don't mind the intrusion. Are we interrupting something?"

"Just finished a letter to my sister. You're just in time for tea, but I suspect you had already figured that out." She glanced at them sideways and disappeared into the kitchen.

Megan and Stacie settled comfortably into their places on the couch. On other occasions they had tried to help Mrs. Barrows fix tea and she had always chased them out of the kitchen, so today they did not even try. They were content to sit and soak up the atmosphere of care and love which exuded from the photographs lining her walls.

"Did you girls go to church this morning?" Mrs. Barrows called out from the kitchen.

"Yes, we did," Stacie answered.

"Someday I hope to come into town and visit your church to thank everyone for their hard work." She came back into the room with a tray filled with the teapot, cups, and pastries. "It means so very much to me to be able to open the camp again, although it will never be the same without David." She poured tea and offered cups to Megan and Stacie.

"Everyone has had a great time with the project, Mrs. Barrows," Megan said. "That's thanks enough."

"I would still like to come." Mrs. Barrows gestured toward their cups. "You girls enjoy your tea, then we'll talk about why you really came to see me."

Megan and Stacie looked at each other.

"We just came because we enjoy your company," Stacie offered weakly.

Mrs. Barrows shook her head. "Are you sure you don't want to talk about yesterday?"

Stacie blushed.

"I saw you and Brad coming out of the woods, you know," Mrs. Barrows said. "It looked to me as if it were more than a casual stroll."

Stacie set her teacup down gently and tried to think of

what to say. "Nothing has really changed, Mrs. Barrows. I'm just not angry with Brad anymore. After all, you were the one who told me I was being unfair and rude to him. I apologized for that."

"Did you tell him you are moving to Weston?" Mrs. Barrows, as usual, was eager to get right to the point.

Stacie looked away, so Megan answered in a chastening voice. "No, she hasn't told him. She doesn't think it will change anything between them."

"I will tell him," Stacie said in her own defense. "I was going to tell him yesterday, but the time was not right."

"More likely you were too frightened," Mrs. Barrows observed. "You're not prepared for how he might respond to the news, are you?"

"I . . . I'm just not sure of what I want," Stacie fudged.

"The Lord works in some strange ways, my dear. Open your eyes and look around you." She leaned forward and took Stacie's hand. "One thing I know for sure: Brad wants you, but he's just as confused as you are."

"But Brad always knows exactly what he wants. He never gets confused."

"Things are not always what they seem to be, Stacie dear."

eleven

Stacie woke the next Saturday to the furor of the rain pelting her window and the entire apartment building shuddering in the wind. The brooding, dark morning sky had made her sleep later than usual, even for a Saturday, until the roar of the storm invaded her unconsciousness and commanded her attention. She got out of bed and went to the window to peer out. The storm was relentless. Pulling her summer robe off its hook in the closet, she wrapped it around herself and padded out to the kitchen to make a pot of coffee.

She was supposed to go out to the camp today to paint. Since it was indoor work, there was no reason to be discouraged by the weather, but she could not help feeling disappointed. The camp was such an invigorating place to spend a day when the weather was nice. Even if the rain let up, after the torrent unleashed last night the pleasant winding walking paths would be reduced once again to slippery trails of mud. Nevertheless, her mood was brightened by the thought that she could see Mrs. Barrows regardless of the weather. The transformation of the run-down structures into solid, safe buildings and the change of the landscape from weed patches to rolling lawns was extremely satisfying, but for Stacie, the highlight of the project had been her growing fondness for Mrs. Barrows. It was hard for her to believe this wise woman and dear friend was a complete stranger only a few weeks ago. She smiled contentedly as she waited for the coffee to brew.

Glad that it was Saturday and she did not have to fight

traffic to get to the office on time, she sat with her feet propped up on the coffee table, sipping her steaming coffee and leisurely flipping through some magazines that had been left unread for weeks. She still had about two hours before she had to leave for the camp, so there was plenty of time to indulge in small pleasures. After a second cup of coffee and a piece of toast, Stacie headed for the shower, where she stood for a very long time under the dense, steamy spray.

At last she emerged, put on her robe, and looked at herself in the mirror. Despite the coffee and magazines and long shower, her face was rippled with strain. The last encounter with Brad had certainly not cleared up any of the confusion she was engulfed in. To complicate matters, Brad had not called all week. There was no objective reason to think he would; nevertheless, she had been reluctantly hopeful.

In the week since she had seen Brad, Stacie had lost a lot of sleep wondering if she should have told him about the job change. Should it make a difference at this point, she wondered. Although he continued to profess his love for her, Brad still had not shown any softening of his position. It was so tempting to let herself surrender to his caresses and live happily ever after married to Brad. But would she be happy? If she took the easy way out and went running back to his arms now—she quickly dismissed the thought. Perhaps she would tell him she would be working in Weston instead of Thomasville, but not yet . . . not until she was completely sure of what the experience of the recent months meant about their relationship.

And what about Dillon. Sweet, charming, attentive Dillon. When she was with Dillon, Stacie almost felt that she could leave her past behind her and start all over again

in a new job in a new city with a new relationship. She felt
no pressure about anything from Dillon; he was simply
comfortable to be with. As much as she would miss her
friends in St. Mary's when she moved, Dillon could make
the change much easier if she would let him.

Stacie towel-dried her hair and began brushing it. The
wind which had awakened her earlier persisted, and once
again she went to the window and stared out. She thought to
herself how truly odd this weather was. It was not a typical
late spring thunderstorm; there was something eerie about
the way the sky looked.

Back out in the living room, Stacie snapped on the television. The usual Saturday morning cartoons dominated the
stations, but she kept flipping channels, hoping to find a
weather report. Suddenly, the set started beeping to signal
the beginning of an emergency report.

*Please be advised that there is a tornado warning cur-
rently in effect for all of Grundman County until 10:00 A.M.
We have received a confirmed report that a tornado has
touched down about twenty miles south of St. Mary's in a
rural area of Grundman County. An abandoned church
camp is said to have the only structures in the immediate
area of touchdown. The extent of the damage is not known.
We repeat, there is a tornado warning currently in effect for
all of Grundman County until 10:00 A.M.*

Stacie was already on the phone, dialing. To her horror,
Mrs. Barrows did not answer. The possibilities raced
through Stacie's mind: Mrs. Barrows could be outside or in
the bathtub, or the phone lines could be down because of the
storm. Or she could be hurt. After twelve haunting rings,
Stacie instinctively dialed Brad's number.

"Hello." His voice sounded muffled.

"Don't they know that camp is not abandoned!" she said, half hysterically. "Mrs. Barrows is out there!"

"Stacie? Is that you? What are you talking about?"

She realized that Brad was probably sleeping late and maybe had not even noticed the rain.

"Brad, there's been a tornado! The guy on television said it touched down in Grundman County at an abandoned church camp. That has to be the Homestead—but they think no one lives there."

"Did you try calling?"

"Of course!" She was impatient with his rationality. Did he think she was a thoughtless idiot? "There's no answer."

"I'm on my way. I'll pick you up in ten minutes."

Stacie hung up the phone and ran to the bedroom to dress. She hurriedly pulled on last night's clothes and twisted her wet hair into a haphazard ponytail. With a rubber poncho pulled over her head, she was out on her front step with an umbrella—which was useless against the wind—when Brad pulled up in his van. He leaned on the horn and stretched across the front seat to throw open the passenger door, and Stacie dashed to the street and hurled herself into the van. She was not sure the vehicle had even come to a complete stop; all she could think about was the danger that Mrs. Barrows might be in.

Normally it took at least forty minutes to drive to the camp, but today the roads were slick and visibility extremely poor. Stacie looked at her watch. It was a little after nine; there was still a danger that the tornado could strike again, and she was leading Brad straight into the heart of it.

"Tell me exactly what they said on television," Brad said, and this time Stacie took comfort in his ability to stay in control and think on his feet.

"It wasn't much. I guess St. Mary's is not in danger, but there's a tornado warning for Grundman County. They said there was a touchdown at an abandoned church camp twenty miles south of town, but no one knows what damage was done."

"How long is the warning in effect?"

"Until ten o'clock. About another hour."

"They may not let us through, Stacie."

"What do you mean? They who? We have to be sure she's all right." Stacie was beside herself with fright. Brad reached over and took a firm hold of her hand.

"It'll be all right, Stace. We'll get to her. But if there's been any damage the county sheriff may have the road to the camp blocked off." He squeezed her hand, and she clutched his arm with her other hand. "We'll get through somehow."

Stacie was beginning to get a grip on her emotions. "Maybe there's something on the radio now," she suggested with surprising calm.

"Good idea." Gently, Brad extricated his hand from her grip so he could work the knobs of the radio. Most of the stations had music or talk shows, but at last he found some news. They impatiently sat through a report of the actions of the state legislature and the governor's vacation plans before finally hearing the information they sought.

A second tornado touchdown has been reported in rural Grundman County, this one allegedly tearing the roof off of a farmhouse and damaging a cornfield. This touchdown is unconfirmed. A religious youth camp believed to be unoccupied may have sustained an unknown amount of damage earlier this morning. In addition, the sheriff's office is reporting that the main roads into Grundman County from the north are subject to flash floods and there may be a power line down. Please avoid driving south into Grundman County. We repeat, avoid driving south into Grundman County.

"Keep going, Brad," Stacie said determinedly, looking directly south.

"I never said I was going to do anything else." Brad looked at his watch. "It's going to take us at least an hour to get there, even if we don't hit a roadblock."

Torrential rains washed across the road with tidal wave force; the wipers running on high speed could hardly keep the windshield clear enough to see the road ahead of them. Brad had both hands tightly on the steering wheel now and was leaning forward, intently focused on staying safely on the pavement. Stacie looked at her watch at least every two minutes as they crept along. They were out of town now and headed into Grundman County. Just as the radio report had said, water swept across the road in many places, and she could not help being frightened by the number of small cars already abandoned along the side of the highway. Brad's van was heavy and high, and so far she felt safe—both in the van and with Brad.

Brad was concentrating much too hard to attempt conversation, but every few minutes, he would say, "It's going to be all right, Stace," and each time she believed him a little more. She prayed silently for Mrs. Barrows and for their own safety as they tried to reach her. Turning her head, she looked at Brad, whose gaze did not leave the road in front of him. In spite of all her confusion about their relationship, she had not hesitated to call him when she needed help. She did not know what the future held for them, but she knew that she loved him and that he loved her. Stacie never had a moment's doubt that he would respond instantly and un-questioningly to her plea simply because she asked.

They came to the narrow, twisting road which would lead them to the camp. There was still another five miles to go, but they were encouraged to have made it this far. Abruptly, Brad slammed on the brakes, and Stacie felt the rear end of the van swing sharply to the right on the slick pavement. A county sheriff's vehicle sat squarely across the road, block-ing any further progress. Brad rolled down his window as the officer approached the van, and Stacie sat forward to hear the conversation.

"You'll have to go back, sir," the officer said. "The creek has risen and the road is flooded just ahead. For your own safety, I have to ask you to turn around."

"What about the camp, officer?" Brad asked calmly. "Do you know how bad the damage is?"

"Not yet. Our emergency crew will get there as soon as possible to assess the damage."

"Sir, are you aware that the camp is not unoccupied? A friend of ours—an elderly woman—is living on the grounds while the camp is being refurbished."

The officer clearly was startled. "Our information was that no one was living there. I'll radio the station immedi-ately and tell them what you said so they can send help. But you'll still have to turn back."

"Of course. Thank you, officer."

Brad obediently rolled up his window and began to nego-tiate a turn in the cramped roadway.

"Bradley! What are you doing?" Stacie demanded. "We can't leave until we know Mrs. Barrows is all right."

"You heard the man. We have to turn back."

"I can't believe my ears. I would never have thought you

would give up so quickly—not when we're this close." Stacie slumped in her seat with disgust and frustration.

"Who said anything about giving up?" Brad said, the van now squared away and headed back toward the main road.

Stacie was confused now. Brad looked at her and winked. Then she started to smile.

"You sly old dog—you know another way, don't you?"

"You guessed it. There's a supply road I used just last week with a truckload of lumber. It's pretty rough, but it'll get us into the camp." He pressed his foot to the accelerator and the van picked up speed.

In only a few minutes he found the turnoff for the supply road. The van bounced from side to side as it hit one pothole after another, but they were making progress. The narrow dirt road was pure mud in places, and even Stacie could feel the tires slipping. Brad doggedly continued; Stacie's knuckles turned white from clenching the dashboard. Even with a seatbelt on, she felt like she could be thrown from her seat with the next lurch.

Without warning, they stopped. "What happened?" Stacie asked urgently, although she already knew the answer.

"There's a tire spinning. We're stuck in the mud, Stacie."

"We're so close! Why is this happening?"

"I can't answer that, but we can't just sit here." Brad looked out the window at the unrelenting downpour. "I'll get out and see what I can do. You sit over here, and when I give you the signal, accelerate."

Stacie thought of Mrs. Barrows and needed no further urging to spring into action. Brad opened the door on his side and hopped down to the mud. She slid over to his seat and twisted around to see what he was doing. She felt the van bouncing as Brad put his weight on the rear bumper and jumped. At his signal, she put her foot on the gas and pushed down gently. The tire continued to spin and Brad was sprayed with mud. The van did not move.

Taking her foot off the pedal, Stacie turned around for Brad's next signal. He spread his feet, gripped the bumper squarely with his hands, then tilted his head at Stacie. Once again she accelerated. This time, the van inched forward until finally she no longer felt the stubborn drag of the mud. Brad charged along the side of the van and jumped in, smearing mud all over Stacie before she could get out of the way. It was with overwhelming relief that Stacie surrendered the steering wheel to Brad.

In another twenty minutes they were at the rear entrance of the camp. Stacie looked at her watch—it was 10:45 A.M. —nearly two hours since the tornado had struck the camp. The rain was letting up at last, but there was no telling what they would find.

"We'll start with the house," Brad said, barreling through the camp road and pulling to a sharp stop in front of the small cottage where Mrs. Barrows lived. Simultaneously they jumped out of the van and ran for the house, calling out her name as loudly as they could.

Stacie tried the front door. "It's open!" she called and pushed her way in. There were only five rooms and it did not take her long to determine that Mrs. Barrows was not in the house. This meant she was out on the grounds somewhere. Stacie ran out the front door, calling for Brad. "She's not here, Brad. She's hurt, I just know it."

"We'll find her, Stacie. She might be fine, just out looking at the damage for herself." Stacie knew he was right—it was completely possible that this is exactly what had happened. But somehow she didn't think so.

"Let's get back in the van," she said, suddenly feeling in control. "Take the outer circle first, past those old cabins we were supposed to paint today."

Brad nodded and complied immediately. The camp road was not built for vehicular traffic, so they had to go slowly. They both looked around carefully for any sign that Mrs. Barrows had been this way recently. They circled around the barn—fortunately there were no animals at the camp yet—and on past the prayer chapel and the open playing field. Constantly they called out her name. The storm had dissipated to a drizzle, making it easier to see and hear, but there was no response to their persistent shouts. Hoping that Brad had been right—that Mrs. Barrows was simply out looking over the grounds now that the storm had passed—Stacie anxiously looked for her friend to peek her head out from around the corner of some building and signal to them that she was safe. But it did not happen, and the further around the circle they went, the stronger was her sense of foreboding danger.

"Stacie, I don't see much damage," Brad said at long last. "There's some fencing missing, but the buildings all seem to be standing."

"So far," Stacie said stubbornly. She had to see for herself that Mrs. Barrows was all right before she would relent.

"Oh no!" Fear was evident in Brad's voice now.

"What?" Stacie cried out in alarm.

"One of the cabins—it's just gone!"

She could see he was right. They were approaching a cluster of four cabins—but only three were standing, surrounded by randomly scattered debris of lumber and bits of furniture.

"We were going to work up here today, Brad," Stacie

said, almost choking on her words. "She might have been up here this morning getting things ready."

Brad halted the van and they got out once more.

"Mrs. Barrows! Margaret! Are you here?" they called out. The silence which answered them was ominous.

Stacie reached for Brad's hand as they began to pick their way through the rubble between the cabins. They looked closely at everything they kicked out of the way. Gradually, they began to bend over and throw aside larger pieces of wood and clear the debris until they could see the ground beneath the piles.

Suddenly, Stacie screamed. Brad was instantly at her side and saw what she pointed to.

Margaret's legs were visible from the knees down beneath a pile of mangled residue of the cabin—but they could see no more of their friend than this. Frantically, they began pulling off the broken chairs and twisted metal bed frames and furiously cast these aside until they could determine what was preventing Mrs. Barrows from standing up.

A beam covered most of her frail body, a large, heavy, long ceiling beam which seemed to be the only piece of the cabin left intact.

Stacie covered her open mouth with one hand and clutched her stomach with the other as Brad began to heave away the last loose pieces. After a split second, she recovered her senses and knelt at Margaret's head and looked carefully at the colorless face.

"She's breathing, Brad, but she's unconscious!"

"Don't try to move her," Brad cautioned. He looked up at Stacie and then at the beam. "I don't think we can move this, Stace," he said mournfully.

"We have to try."

"Of course we'll try. But I really think we're going to need help."

Together they tried to find a point of leverage and lift the beam off of Mrs. Barrows. Brad's muscles rippled with perspiration as he pushed and pulled to the extent of his strength. With growing dread Stacie realized they could not budge the beam even an inch; it was futile to think they might, and they were wasting precious time trying.

"You're right, Brad, we need help. At least we know she's alive. I could kick myself now, but I didn't think to check to see if the phone was working when I went through the house."

"We've got to get through to the sheriff's office and tell them to get medical help out here immediately. I'll take the van and go back to the house. If I'm not back in a few minutes, it means the phone is dead and I had to go find that officer at the roadblock."

Stacie nodded at the sensibility of his plan. Tears were streaming down her cheeks. She was terrified, but she had with her the one person she most wanted to be near in a crisis. Even when he left her alone with the unconscious Mrs. Barrows, she knew she would draw strength from him.

Brad came to where she sat on the wet ground near Margaret's head and squatted down next to her. "Will you be all right?"

"I have to be," she responded, almost on the verge of sobbing. "Hurry, Brad. Go, and hurry back."

twelve

Stacie dared not touch Mrs. Barrows. Every muscle in her body screamed to reach out and wrap itself around the woman lying unconscious in the rubble. But she held back, anxiously waiting for Brad to come back with medical help who would know whether Mrs. Barrows could be moved safely. Although Margaret was already drenched, Stacie pulled off her rain poncho and gently spread it over the still form. Desperately she wished she had some warm blankets to wrap around Mrs. Barrows. She knew there were some in the cottage, but she was afraid to leave her helpless friend alone long enough to run for them. Stacie whimpered as she watched vigilantly for any sign of consciousness. There was none.

Stacie rummaged through her pockets and came up with a tissue. Delicately, she wiped the grime from Mrs. Barrows's face. For the first time, she noticed that the older woman's glasses were missing. Stacie instinctively glanced around to see if they were in sight, but it was hopeless to try to find them. Undoubtedly they were broken anyway. Without them, Mrs. Barrows did not look herself. Instead of her bright blue eyes, Stacie saw only sagging, still eyelids. Her colorless skin made Stacie gasp in a moment of fright. She bent her head close to Mrs. Barrows's mouth to listen. The shallow sound she heard brought instant relief; Mrs. Barrows was not breathing deeply, but she was breathing. Without disturbing her position, Stacie reached for a wrist and felt for a heartbeat. Once again she was relieved.

She looked at her watch. How long had Brad been gone?

Only five minutes—it seemed so much longer. Cold and wet, she crouched and tried to keep warm. Was it only six days ago that she and Megan had indulged in their spontaneous picnic and descended on Margaret for tea? She had been her usual vivacious self, fussing over the teapot, insisting that they eat pastries, and offering advice they did not even know they wanted. Despite her age, Stacie had never once thought of Mrs. Barrows as fragile or delicate. But now there was no strength left in her. In fact, she looked as if she might slip away at any moment. The stark contrast between that delightful day last weekend and the dreadful sight before her was too much for Stacie and her whimpers swelled to sobs.

The sound of groaning startled her. She looked down to see Mrs. Barrows trying to turn her head.

"What . . . happened. . . ." the older woman sighed.

"Shhh," Stacie soothed her, stroking her forehead. "Brad went for help."

"Stacie . . . is that you?" Mrs. Barrows still had not opened her eyes, and her voice was barely audible.

"Yes, it's me." Stacie was encouraged that her voice had been recognized. "Just lie still until Brad gets back." The control in her voice did not betray the magnitude of her relief that Mrs. Barrows had risen to consciousness and was able to speak coherently.

"I came out . . . to the cabins . . . paint . . . storm . . . happened so fast."

"Please, Margaret, don't try to talk. Please just be still until we get some help." Stacie wiped her face off again. "I'm sorry I don't have anything to keep you warmer."

"How . . . did you get . . . here? The road. . . ."

"Yes, the road was flooded, but Brad knew another way in. We had to see if you were all right."

"I . . . I. . . ." Mrs. Barrows was drifting away.

"Margaret! Mrs. Barrows! Don't go to sleep. I think you should try to stay awake."

"Can't. . . ." To Stacie's dismay, Mrs. Barrows lapsed into unconsciousness again.

Brad had been gone more than ten minutes now. That meant the phone in the cottage was not working and he had gone out to the road. Maybe he could not even get through; they had barely been able to drive in on the back road.

"Dear Lord, please let him get through," Stacie prayed aloud. Wiping streaks of tears from her face, she continued to pray steadily, never taking her eyes off of Mrs. Barrows.

It was another ten minutes before Stacie heard the roar of the van's engine coming down the camp road. Brad screeched to a halt and leaped out. As he ran toward Stacie, he called out, "How is she? Is she still alive?"

Stacie choked on a sob and nodded vigorously. "Yes. She was conscious for a few minutes. I tried to keep her awake, but. . . ."

She stood up and threw her arms around Brad's neck, clutching tightly. He stroked the back of her head to soothe her.

"Did you find anyone to help us?" she asked.

"Yes. But I had to go all the way out to that trooper who wanted us to turn around." He held her close. "He used the radio to call for help. The paramedics are on the way."

"The road—"

"It's muddy, but it's clear," he assured her. "Stacie, you're shivering. Sit down over here and try to keep warm."

She did not want to let go of him, but she obeyed his instructions, shaking both from chill and fright.

"I've got a couple of old blankets in the van. Will you be all right while I get them?"

She nodded tearfully, and he ran back to where he had left the van. She watched him go, admiring his strength in contrast to her own collapse at the sight of Mrs. Barrows under the beam. It was so typical of Brad to be unruffled no matter how severe the problem.

Throughout the two years they dated and the months of their engagement, Brad had always been a rock. In some ways Stacie knew she had depended on him too much. He was quick to make decisions, while she could spend weeks weighing the pros and cons of every little choice. She had to admit that his decisions were usually good ones. Maybe it had been a good decision to break their engagement instead of facing the dilemma of a marriage spread out over 200 miles.

Stacie thought of herself as intelligent and competent. Obviously Jack Rogers and Dillon Graves saw her that way as well. Her work was compassionate and insightful, and she had a way of helping people feel at ease. She was a great organizer and threw herself wholeheartedly into everything she did. But when it came to Brad, her mind turned to mush; she could not think clearly or define her feelings for him.

Brad returned with two tattered blankets; Stacie jumped up to spread one over Mrs. Barrows. She tucked it in around her bony form as snugly as she could without causing movement. As Stacie stooped and lightly stroked the hair of her newest friend, Brad crouched beside her and wrapped a torn army blanket around her shoulders. Instantly she felt warmer, though she knew the dampness of her clothing would soon seep through the green wool. She let her weight rest against his chest and welcomed his arms around her. Together they silently watched Mrs. Barrows for any sign of change, for good or for worse.

The screeching siren announced the arrival of the ambulance. They both jumped to their feet and hurried up to greet it, waving their hands wildly to show their location as it came around the circle. The siren went silent and two paramedics jumped out of the front seat.

"We almost didn't find this place," the driver said. "That supply road is not on my map. Whoever gave directions did a great job."

Stacie looked at Brad and could not help feeling proud. Without his clear thinking, it could have taken much longer for help to arrive.

The paramedics, garbed in blue uniforms and yellow slickers, were already at work on Mrs. Barrows.

"Vital signs are good, all things considered," remarked one as he set up the radio to communicate with the hospital. "She seems to still have circulation to the legs. That's good. We'll get an I.V. started and then we'll see about getting this beam moved."

"The fire department is right behind us," said the driver. "They'll wrap a chain around this thing and lift it off in no time."

As if fulfilling his prediction, another siren screamed into the camp as a red fire truck lumbered through the narrow road. Three more men in yellow slickers jumped down and went into action. A small crane on the back of the truck wheeled around and the men churned chain off an enormous spool. Brad moved quickly to help fasten it around the beam, while Stacie held her position next to Mrs. Barrows's head. Faster than Stacie could have imagined, the beam rose in the air, swung around, and crashed into the pile that had been the cabin. Stacie was horrified at the sight of Mrs. Barrows's crushed legs. Obviously, they were both broken; she had known all along that they must be, but it was terrifying to see that it was true. Mrs. Barrows was probably unconscious because of the pain.

The paramedic, expertly slid a stretcher under Mrs. Barrows, still unconscious, and hoisted her into the ambulance. The driver turned to Stacie as he raced around to the front seat. "Are you coming along to the hospital?" he asked.

"Yes!" she cried, and immediately lurched toward the back of the vehicle, still clutching the army blanket around her shoulders. She looked at Brad over one shoulder.

"Go ahead," he said, helping her into the ambulance. "I'll bring the van in and meet you at the hospital."

She nodded as the second paramedic jumped in and swung the doors shut, harshly leaving Brad on the outside.

The siren shrieked again as the ambulance plowed through the mud and began its journey to the hospital in St. Mary's.

Stacie stopped for a moment to lean against the wall in the emergency room. It was the middle of the afternoon, and she was sore and tired and emotionally worn out, not to mention sopping wet. Her clothes, muddy from her vigil at the side of Mrs. Barrows, stuck to her body, and she longed to peel them off and step into a hot shower. She had been at the hospital for more than two hours. As soon as the doctor took a look at Mrs. Barrows, he had shooed Stacie out of the examining room and left her to wait for what seemed an eternity before finally reporting on Margaret's condition.

Stacie still had not connected with Brad. Surely he had followed the ambulance to the hospital, just as he said he would. Probably he had not been allowed beyond the waiting room of the emergency room. Since she was not immediate family, even Stacie had been only grudgingly tolerated outside the examining room. She rubbed her eyes with the dirty heels of her hands and decided to find Brad. If he were waiting someplace where they could not tell him what was happening, he would be worried sick.

After pausing to get a drink of cold water from the fountain, Stacie pushed open the doors that led to the reception area for the emergency room. To her amazement there were four people there from the church, among them, Megan.

Megan spotted Stacie and quickly crossed the room; the others were not far behind. "What's going on?" she asked. "How is she?" She put her arm around Stacie's damp shoulders.

"She's in bad shape, but they think she'll be all right. Both of her legs are broken, and some ribs are cracked." She looked wearily around the group. "The main thing is that she is still unconscious. Except for a few minutes after we first found her, she hasn't regained consciousness at all. They're not sure why." The ponytail she had pulled her hair into so many hours ago had given way. Now, she pressed a damp strand of hair back from her face, but it refused her effort and drooped down over one eye. "There's nothing we can do. I'm sure they'll let us know if there's any change."

Stacie still carried her rain poncho and Brad's two blankets. She looked around. "Where's Brad? Isn't he here?"

Megan took the damp pile out of Stacie's arms. "He's around here somewhere." She tried to fold the blankets a little more neatly and then stacked them on the floor. "You need some dry clothes, Stacie. Why don't you let me take you home to change."

Stacie shook her head defiantly. "No. I'm staying."

Megan backed off. "Okay, then how about if you give me your key and let me go to your place for some dry clothes. I can be back in half an hour."

This time Stacie nodded and dug in her jeans pockets for her apartment key. Gratefully, she handed it to Megan.

"I'll get a towel, too," Megan said sensibly. "You can clean up in the ladies' room."

Megan left and Stacie sank into the nearest chair, exhausted. Others from the group tried to talk to her, but she did not feel much like having a conversation and left many of their questions unanswered. She dared not lean her head back against the wall for fear of falling asleep, which she did not want to do until she knew Margaret was all right. Where was Brad, she wondered again.

Then she saw him. He came in from the hall with a cup of coffee in his hand—and Jenna McLean at his side. Stacie turned her head and looked away. She remembered Brad's explanation of Jenna's attentiveness, and she believed him completely, but she was not much in the mood to encounter it first hand.

Brad came directly across the room and stood in front of Stacie. Setting his coffee cup down, he reached for her hands and pulled her to her feet. He was as muddy and damp as she was, but neither of them cared. She fell into his embrace and buried her head against his chest, oblivious to the surprised audience around them. They stood like that for several minutes, not wanting to let go of one another. Finally, Brad steered her toward a sagging couch where they could sit together and continue to comfort each other.

Out of the corner of one eye, Stacie could see Jenna McLean sitting by herself, swinging one foot in a nervous rhythm. But she knew the truth about Jenna now and did not feel threatened by her. It was up to Brad to make Jenna understand where things stood between them, and Stacie instinctively knew not to get involved.

No matter what the future held for the relationship between Brad and Stacie, she was glad he was there in that room at that moment. If he had not been home this morning when she phoned, she would have panicked. He had been a tower of strength all day, and she did not want to suffer through this ordeal without him.

But she could not think beyond the moment. She blocked out the larger questions which plagued her recently; this was not the time or place to try to sort them out.

Megan returned with a plastic bag containing a complete change of clothing. Insistently, she pried Stacie away from Brad and escorted her down the hall.

"Come over here, Stacie," Megan instructed, turning on the water and splashing her hand under the hot water. "This won't be the same as a real bath, but you'll feel better."

"The only thing that will make me feel better is hearing that Margaret is okay," replied Stacie.

Satisfied with the water temperature, Megan pulled up the stopper and let the sink fill up. "If it weren't for you, she might not even be alive, Stace."

"Why is she still unconscious?" Stacie stepped up to the sink and splashed hot water on her face and arms while Megan took the dry clothes out of the plastic bag.

"At least her vital signs are good, right?"

"I should have tried harder to keep her awake."

"You did everything you could, Stacie. Stop beating yourself up." Megan handed Stacie a towel and the clothes and told her to change in one of the stalls.

Cleaner and dryer, Stacie did feel a little better. Brad sat where she had left him, still damp but not seeming to care about his own condition. She sat down beside him and willingly took hold of his hand. Megan bundled up all the wet clothes and blankets and said she would take them out to her car.

"She's like a mother hen, the way she looks after me," Stacie commented.

Brad smiled slightly. "It comes from hanging around five-year-olds all the time like she does. She can't stop taking care of people."

Momentarily relaxed, Stacie leaned her head on Brad's shoulder.

Jenna nonchalantly wandered across the room and sat across from them. Stacie smiled pleasantly but decided not to say anything.

After a few minutes, Jenna spoke. "Brad, maybe you'd like to go get something from the cafeteria. I'll bet you haven't eaten all day."

Brad's response was even and firm. "No thanks, Jenna. I'm fine for now." His fingers tightened their hold on Stacie's.

Stacie sensed the disappointment Jenna was feeling but returned Brad's warm grasp. She felt a twinge of guilt, since she knew that she was relying on Brad's stamina for the moment without being sure what their relationship would be like tomorrow or next week. But she needed Brad right now. Besides, Brad had already told her that he was not interested in Jenna McLean.

More than once during the afternoon, Stacie found herself checking her watch against the clock on the waiting room wall, thinking surely that time was standing still. The minute hand circled slowly around its route, dragging the hour hand with it. Megan made several trips to the cafeteria for coffee and kept everyone well supplied. Despite Brad's rebuffing, Jenna stayed with the group, and Stacie believed she was sincerely concerned about Mrs. Barrows. What she could not believe was how slowly time was passing. Every magazine in the room had been passed around to each of them at least once. Every crack in the paint, every flaw in the furniture became all too familiar to Stacie. Other people waiting for other patients came and went, and the vigil for Margaret Barrows continued.

Every time the automatic emergency room doors swished open, Stacie's heart skipped a beat. When Dr. Pressman finally appeared, she was instantly on her feet.

"How is she, Doctor?" she asked, hardly giving him a chance to speak. "Is she conscious? Can I see her?"

"Slow down, Stacie," the doctor said, holding his hand up in the air. "She's better and yes, she is conscious. I'm sure now that she is out of the woods. At her age, we'll have to keep a close watch on how the broken bones heal, but she seems to be in good health generally, so we have every reason to believe she will heal completely."

The group gave up a mass sigh of relief, and Dr. Pressman continued his report.

"She's resting comfortably, and she asked about you, Stacie, but I must insist that she be allowed complete rest tonight." He looked around at the group. "Obviously you all care about her a great deal, but the best thing you can do now is go home and get some rest yourselves, especially you, Stacie. Come back tomorrow—just one or two at a time, please."

With that, Dr. Pressman turned around and disappeared into the emergency room once again. The group looked at each other and slowly started for the door. Stacie looked from Brad to Megan, grateful that they were both there.

Brad put his arm around her shoulders. "Come on, Stace. I'll take you home."

Stacie did not resist the suggestion. Megan walked out with them, and when they reached her car, Stacie gave her a quick hug and whispered thanks before continuing on to Brad's van.

The once, shiny van was splattered with mud, both inside and out. It was starting to drizzle again, but not hard enough to wash off the dirt, only enough to smear it around. Stacie could hardly see out her side of the windshield, so she was not surprised when Brad took the time to clean it off properly. She leaned her head back against the seat and watched absently as he worked. Before today she had never even been in Brad's new van. For months, she had listened to his plans to buy one and looked at brochures and reports with him. But he did not buy it until after they split up, so this was the first time to share his fulfilled dream. She was sorry it was under such oppressive circumstances. She scanned the dashboard and saw that it had all the features he wanted, with plenty of room in the back for transporting tools and supplies for his work. He had made a good choice, she decided.

Brad climbed into the driver's seat and smiled at her while he turned the ignition key. They did not speak much during the ride home, but even the silence between them was comforting. The scenery around them however, was alarming. Apparently no buildings in town had been affected by the tornado itself, but the fierce winds had ripped trees from their roots and strewn them around the neighborhoods. Large branches of older trees hung precariously, ready to fall with the next storm. At this point in the day, Stacie was too numb to absorb the impact the storm had had on the town itself.

Parked in front of her apartment, Brad came around and opened Stacie's door. As he walked her to the door, he said, "I'm glad you called me this morning, Stace. The way things have been between us, I didn't know what to expect."

Stacie shrugged. "What we've been going through is inconsequential compared to what happened today. Mrs. Barrows is all that matters."

Brad nodded. "I won't argue with you there." He paused, and she thought he was going to kiss her, but he didn't. He just squeezed her hand and said, "Good night, Stacie. I'll call you."

"Good night, Brad," she murmured, surprised. She had imagined he would come into the apartment with her, but he had already turned to walk back to the van.

She let herself into her apartment and immediately went into the bathroom to start a proper bath. She rummaged under the sink and came up with a couple of ounces of bubble bath and poured it under the running water. She watched, mesmerized, as the foam multiplied and swelled to an inviting crest. When she shut off the water, she also shut off the light and lowered herself into the tub in the dark. She could not remember the last time her entire body felt so sore. Perhaps it was when her mother died. Stacie, who was nineteen at the time, had been frightened then, too, but she had not had anyone like Brad to lean on. She had been on her own with her grief then, and she never wanted to do that again. She never wanted to be that alone again.

Obviously she loved Brad. But what she and Megan had talked about last weekend was haunting her. *Could she trust Brad? Could she love him unreservedly, or would she always be afraid that she would come second to his other goals?* Stacie consciously set these thoughts aside for another time. In contrast to the taxing day, she was starting to relax in the hot bath and gave herself over to enjoying it completely.

thirteen

Stacie's arms were so full she almost could not get the door open. Unsuccessful at using her elbows to open the door of the hospital gift shop, she turned around and backed into it, giving it a shove with one hip. The glass door finally opened and Stacie entered the main lobby, her arms laden with books and a potted Swedish ivy plant.

In the lobby, she stood still for a moment to get her bearings; for some reason, it was easy for her to get turned around in this hospital. She always had to concentrate on following the blue floor stripe down the gray-tiled hall to the elevator. Cautiously, she balanced her load in one arm so she could free up a finger to push the button of the elevator. While she waited for the muted ding to announce the arrival of the elevator, Stacie relaxed. The appealing color scheme of the hospital—gray, blue, and mauve—was very restful.

Every day for the last ten days, Stacie had stopped by the hospital on her way home from work. Despite assurances from the doctor, she wanted to see for herself that Margaret Barrows was getting better. An eighty-three-year-old woman with two broken legs was not something to take lightly. Nearly every night, images of Margaret lying cold and still in the rain haunted Stacie's sleep. So every afternoon she went to the hospital to see that Margaret was really warm and lively, just the way she had always been, even though she was confined to a bed.

Stacie rode up to the fourth floor and found room 477. Before entering, she paused to listen for voices. She heard only the quiet background sound of the bedside radio so she knocked briskly and went in.

"Hello, Mrs. Barrows. How's my favorite patient today?"

"Quite chipper, thank you." Margaret inspected Stacie's full arms. "What in the world have you got there?"

Stacie lifted the plant a little higher. "I went in for a magazine and came out with three books and a plant." She shrugged her shoulders. "I'm an easy target when it comes to greenery. I thought you might enjoy having it here in your room."

"That's very thoughtful, dear, and the plant is lovely. I'm not quite sure where you are going to put it, though."

Stacie was already scanning the room. In typical hospital fashion, the furnishings were sparse, but the heating vent running across one end of the room doubled as a countertop. The limited space was already cluttered with nearly three dozen cards from well-wishers and a bouquet of cut flowers that were starting to wilt. Stacie cleared a space for the plant by moving the vase to one side and rearranging several of the cards.

"Everyone has been so kind," Mrs. Barrows said. "Especially you, Stacie. You needn't come absolutely every day, you know."

Stacie turned to the bed and took Margaret's hand. "Stop scolding me!" she said in mock irritation. "I will be here every day whether you like it or not."

"It just so happens that I do like it," Mrs. Barrows assured her. "May I change the subject? I understand things are going well at the camp. I had a note from Donna about the publicity."

"Yes, she's coordinating the registrations. We've had a good response from the other churches. The weekend camps are filling up quickly and we have the counselors lined up, so we think it will work out."

"What about someone to cook? I'm afraid I won't be of much use in the kitchen for quite some time."

Stacie squeezed Margaret's hand. "Megan's working out a schedule for people to take turns cooking. Don't worry; the kids will not go hungry."

"In one of those upper cabinets in the dining hall, there is a cookbook I used to use. It might help Megan if she could see it. Feeding sixty kids at a time is not easy, you know."

Stacie nodded. "I'll look for it. But please don't worry about it. We'll be ready on time."

"Will you be there for opening day, Stacie?"

"I think so. I don't start working in Weston until the next week." She propped herself on the edge of the bed more securely. "Weston is not that far away; I'm sure I'll make it down a couple of times during the summer."

"You just missed Brad, you know."

Stacie smiled. "You're changing the subject again. We were talking about the camp."

"You were talking about Weston," Margaret corrected her, "and I have the distinct feeling that you still have not discussed that with Brad."

"Why don't I get you some fresh water." Stacie picked up the brown plastic pitcher and stepped toward the sink.

"You can waffle all you want, Stacie Hanaken, but you can't change the facts." Margaret's voice was very stern. "You haven't spoken to him about it, have you?"

Stacie abandoned her diversionary tactic and set the pitcher back on the night stand, still empty. "I just never think it's the right time."

"You just never have enough courage."

Stacie had no answer. As usual, Margaret Barrows went to the heart of the question. At least half of the time when Stacie came to the hospital, Brad was there, too. Several times they had walked out to the parking lot together. They were comfortable with each other, even affectionate, but they had not talked about anything other than Mrs. Barrows or the work at the camp. On the days when Stacie pulled into the parking lot and saw Brad's van parked, her hands got clammy and her heartbeat quickened. Inwardly, she scolded herself for acting like a schoolgirl with a crush, but she could not deny that being near Brad made her feel something that no one else in her life evoked. Secretly, each time she came, she hoped to find him visiting Margaret.

Yet, she kept him at arm's length. She avoided talking about her job or moving to Weston. And if she sensed that he was about to say something that probed their relationship, she quickly steered the conversation to lighter subjects and focused her attention on anything other than his gaze. Sometimes she could feel him watching her when they were together at the hospital; and she could nearly feel the sensation of his arms around her and the closeness they had shared on the day of the tornado. But she drew very clear boundaries around their relationship.

What was she afraid of? Clearly Brad wanted to reestablish their relationship and clearly her feelings were equally strong. *So what was holding her back?* Only a few weeks ago, she found it difficult to be around him. Now she looked forward to seeing him, but she did not dare let him know. *Why couldn't she abandon her hesitations and at least tell him about Weston?* That would be a starting point to find out if their relationship had a future. *But was she ready to find out about the future?*

"I'm sure you think I'm a crabby old woman who doesn't know how to mind her own business."

Margaret's words brought Stacie back to the present conversation. "No, of course not," she was quick to answer. "I always appreciate your advice."

"Forget the advice. Let me remind you of a story I'm sure you already know—Abraham and the sacrifice of Isaac."

"I'm not sure I follow," Stacie said cautiously.

"Think of yourself as Abraham and Brad as Isaac. I'm sure you will see my point."

Stacie pondered this silently. God asked Abraham to sacrifice Isaac his son, and Abraham was obedient enough to do it. In the end, God gave him back Isaac the very thing he was supposed to give up.

"It's time for your pills again, Mrs. B."

Stacie looked up to see the head nurse breeze into the room with a small paper cup in her hand.

"I feel absolutely fine," Mrs. Barrows announced. "I don't believe I need any pills today."

The nurse rattled the pills in the cup. "Doctor's orders, Mrs. B. When the doctor does his rounds in the morning, you can talk to him about it. Until then. . . ."

"You do what the doctor says," Stacie warned, shaking her finger. "I'm going to sit right here until I see you swallow those pills."

"Oh, all right." Obviously, Mrs. Barrows was outvoted. "But I feel so much better. I fail to see why I am even here."

"Mrs. B, in case you haven't noticed, you have two broken legs. And your ribs are pretty banged up, too." The nurse softened a bit and added, "Actually, we all agree that you are doing very well. I think the doctor might be ready to release you soon, but we're concerned because you live alone out in the country. Maybe a few weeks in a rest home—"

Margaret cut her off. "Oh, that does not sound appealing in the least. I may be an old lady, but I'm as sensible as I ever have been. I've already worked it out so I won't be alone when I go home."

The nurse lifted an eyebrow in interest. "Oh? Perhaps you should talk to the doctor about it tomorrow, then." She handed Mrs. Barrows the little cup with the pills. "In the meantime, you must take these."

Mrs. Barrows grimaced, but she took the pills and swallowed them. Satisfied, the nurse left them to their conversation.

"You know, Stacie," Mrs. Barrows said, "I spent a lot of time waiting around this hospital when David was ill, but, before now, I've never been a patient. I don't care for it very much. I am not accustomed to people fussing over me all day long."

"They're just following doctor's orders and taking good care of you," Stacie reminded her. "Now tell me what you meant when you said you would not be alone when you went home."

"Bradley! I thought you had gone." Mrs. Barrows left Stacie's question unanswered and looked past her to the doorway filled with Brad's tall frame.

"I left my jacket." He gestured to a chair where his blue windbreaker was slung carelessly over the back. "Hi, Stacie. I thought you might be here. I came a little earlier today, so I missed you."

Stacie smiled warmly at Brad. He was in his work clothes and no doubt had come straight from his construction site. But he had made an effort to clean up. His tee shirt was neatly tucked into his jeans and his wavy hair was freshly combed. He needed a haircut, but Stacie found the ragged look appealing. Even when he was dirty and tired, she wanted to be near him. She followed every movement he made as he swept up his jacket with one hand and turned to look at her. Out of the corner of her eye, Stacie could see Mrs. Barrows looking back and forth between her and Brad. The color rose in Stacie's cheeks. Neither she nor Brad spoke, but they looked steadily at each other with slight smiles on their lips.

"They'll be bringing my dinner very soon," Mrs. Barrows said. "I'm sure the two of you could use a cup of coffee at the very least. Why don't you go down to the cafeteria and see what you can do to remedy that?"

Mrs. Barrows made no attempt to hide her pleasure at seeing the two of them together. Her directness momentarily embarrassed Stacie, who broke her gaze on Brad and instead glanced nervously out the window. She fumbled for words. "Oh, I'm sure Brad is busy. He's already late because he forgot his jacket. . . ."

Brad was chuckling. "Don't waste your breath, Stacie. The only way she'll be satisfied is if we agree to go down to the cafeteria together. So just give in and agree."

Stacie relaxed and laughed, too. "All right. But just coffee—you know what the food is like down there." She leaned over and gave Mrs. Barrows a quick kiss on the cheek. "I'll see you tomorrow."

Brad and Stacie walked down the hall together toward the elevator.

"I've been meaning to call you, Stacie," Brad said apologetically. "But I've been so busy since the weather got nice. There's a lot of outdoor work to be done this time of year."

"I'm sure you're swamped with work. At least everything is under control at the camp, so you don't have to worry about that." She pushed the elevator button and absently looked up at the numbered lights above the door.

"What I mean to say," Brad said, groping for words, "is that I was hoping we could spend some time together before you move away. I know you want to take things slow and easy—and that's fine—but I'd like to know where things stand."

The doors slipped open and they stepped into the empty elevator.

"I'm sorry to be causing so much confusion. . . ." One level of Stacie's mind was concentrating hard on keeping up with this conversation; at another level, she grappled with how to tell him she was not moving very far away. If she had any hope of having what she had sacrificed, then surely this was the moment.

Brad was talking, and she was missing part of his words. She snapped back to attention. "I've done my share of confusing things," he said.

The elevator came to a smooth stop on the first floor. Stacie saw the white block letters directing them to the cafeteria, and she wavered for a moment.

"Brad, I don't really want any coffee. Would you mind if we just walked for a bit?"

Brad lifted his wrist and looked at his watch. "I have a meeting in a few minutes, actually. How about if I walk you to your car at least."

Stacie nodded. She wanted to tell him about Weston. His being in a hurry would make it easy to let the moment pass and keep putting it off, but in the elevator she had resolved to do it now. He held open the outside door for her. By the time her shoes hit the sidewalk, she had decided she could not wait any longer.

"Brad, I'm not moving to Thomasville."

Her abrupt words had a jarring effect. Brad stopped in the middle of the doorway and looked at her, bewildered.

Quickly, she continued her explanation. "I'm still taking the new job, but the location has changed. We're going to open a shelter in Weston instead of Thomasville."

"I see." Brad continued walking.

Brad's terse reply surprised Stacie. She waited for him to say more, but he gave no indication that he would say anything. Along with Megan and Margaret Barrows, Stacie had always supposed that when she told Brad she was not moving to Thomasville, he would be enthusiastic and want to resume their engagement. Mentally, she had prepared herself to remind him that this one change in her job did not resolve all their problems. Although she had procrastinated about having this discussion, she had played it out in her mind over and over again, always assuming Brad's response.

But she had been wrong. Brad did not say any of the things she thought he would say. Her carefully prepared defenses were unnecessary. She had supposed that he would take her in his arms and tell her he loved her, but he made no move even to touch her hand.

After an awkward silence, Stacie changed the subject. "My car is over this way."

Brad walked stiffly beside her. She spotted his van, so she knew that he was going out of his way to walk her to her car. When she first suggested that they take a walk, she had imagined a more extended conversation—and some reaction to her news. She did not know what to make of his silent response.

She opened the car door and turned to him, determined to make one last attempt. "I'll still be around for a couple of weeks. We could get together. . . ."

Brad nodded but still did not say anything.

"Well, you'd better get to your meeting," Stacie said awkwardly. "Good night, Brad."

"Good night, Stacie. Have a nice evening." His tone was courteous and warm, but there was no spark. Stacie might as well have been a salesclerk in the local department store.

fourteen

Stacie closed the folder and pushed it to the corner of her desk. Three more awaited her attention.

All afternoon she had been making her way through a stack of case files, updating the information and writing brief notes so the new caseworker would know the status of each file. There was not much to say really. Especially in recent weeks, a lot of her time had been spent on research and reports; she missed being actively involved with families in need. Working in Weston would put her in direct contact with as many as twelve families at a time, and she was looking forward to that dimension of the job. She still had a lot to learn, but she was eager to start learning it by actually doing the work of helping families get back on their feet.

She stretched her arms out in front of her and yawned. Since leaving Brad in the parking lot four days ago, she had felt unsettled and had not slept well. The lack of sleep was catching up with her but it was Friday, and she looked forward to sleeping late tomorrow morning. She patted her open mouth with the fingers of one hand as another yawn forced itself out.

"I saw that."

Stacie flinched, startled by the voice in her doorway.

"What's the matter, Stacie? Are you working all night or something?"

"Dillon! Marsha didn't tell me you were coming." Stacie's mind scrambled for an explanation of his presence.

"That's because Marsha didn't know. It was kind of an

158

impulsive thing." He lowered his slender frame into the chair across from her desk and gave her a friendly look. "Besides, I didn't come to see Marsha, as charming as she is. I came to see you."

Stacie looked at him quizzically. "Have I forgotten a meeting or something? Sometimes my brain doesn't work too well on Fridays," she said apologetically.

"Nah, no meeting. I just wanted to see you."

Stacie reached into her desk drawer for the file on the Weston building. "I'm sure there are some things we need to discuss. I'm still waiting to hear from a couple of people—"

"It's Friday afternoon, Stacie." Dillon interrupted her. "I didn't drive 200 miles on a Friday afternoon to talk about the building."

"Excuse me?" Intuitively, Stacie was on guard.

"When I phoned you a couple of weeks ago, you said you had some people at your place and couldn't talk."

Stacie nodded. "Yes. That was the night we were planning publicity for the camp."

"But you never called me back. I've left several messages on your machine."

Stacie looked away. How could she possibly explain to Dillon everything that had happened in the last few weeks— or even in the last few days. The truth was that she had not thought about her personal relationship with him very much lately.

"This may sound like a trite excuse," she began, "but I've been taking care of a sick friend. Mrs. Barrows, the woman who owns the camp, was injured when a cabin collapsed. She's eighty-three years old, and I've been really worried about her."

"I'm sorry to hear about that." Dillon looked genuinely

sympathetic. "I hope she's getting better. But you look like you could really use a break, some time to relax. How about spending the day with me tomorrow?"

Stacie ran her hand through her hair, stalling for time. There was not much to be done at the camp anymore, but she had been planning to spend Saturday alone, catching up on her reading and writing long overdue letters.

Dillon sensed her hesitation. "I know it's short notice, and you probably have a thousand things you could be doing with a day off. But I'd really like it if you spent it with me."

What was really holding her back was too complicated to explain. In the past, being with Dillon allowed her to detach from the pressure she felt about other things in her life. He was completely separate from her existence in St. Mary's and he had no idea what her life was really like.

Against her better judgment, she said, "Okay, sure. It would be nice to get away from things."

"They're forecasting nice weather; maybe we could go to the zoo," Dillon suggested.

Stacie nodded. "I haven't been there for a couple of years. That would be great."

Dillon stood up. "Looks like you've got a lot of work to wade through, so I'll get out of your way. I'll let you sleep in tomorrow and pick you up in the late morning, if that's all right."

"That would be perfect," Stacie answered, smiling.

After Dillon was gone, Stacie had a hard time concentrating. It was a good thing the day was already nearly over. She did not make much progress with the rest of the files and was relieved when 5:00 P.M. finally came.

At home, she dropped her briefcase on the coffee table and plopped down on the couch, wondering what in the world she had gotten herself into now. *Why had she accepted a date with Dillon? Weren't things complicated enough with Brad right now?* She reminded herself that Dillon did not know anything about Brad; and she had certainly acted interested in Dillon the last time they were together. She really did enjoy being with him, but the change in her relationship with Brad during the last three weeks certainly affected her perspective. And this was all at Dillon's expense. He was entitled to some explanation. Once again she was being unfair to someone she cared about.

It's not really a date, she told herself; it's just two friends going to the zoo to enjoy a nice day. The zoo would be a public place with a lot to see and do; maybe being with Dillon would help her sort things out once and for all.

The next morning, the sun woke her up much earlier than she would have liked, but she indulged in the luxury of lying in bed in that half-awake state where her problems did not seem real. Periodically, she would turn over or bury her face in the pillow at a new angle. Burdened with the dilemma of what to do about Dillon, she had not slept well—again.

Eventually, she got up and made coffee. Leisurely, she looked at the morning newspaper. It was past 9:00 A.M. before she decided to get started on some of the things she wanted to do before Dillon came. Dishes had been stacking up in the sink for three days, and she could not remember the last time she had dusted and vacuumed. She certainly did not want anyone to see the apartment looking that way, and, if she hurried, maybe she could get a load of laundry done before he arrived. She decided to get the work done first and then shower and dress properly. Revitalized by coffee and toast, she shifted into an active mode. She pulled on some comfortable sweats, tied her hair back with a ragged ribbon, and got started.

She cleared up the dirty dishes, inventoried her refrigerator, and made a grocery list. She had just gotten the vacuum cleaner out of the closet when the doorbell rang. Without even thinking about who it might be, she went to the door and pulled it open automatically.

"Dillon!"

He looked at her, amused. "You didn't forget our date, did you?"

"No, of course not," she said, stepping aside so he could come in. "I'm sorry. . . . I wasn't. . . . What time is it?"

Dillon started to laugh, and Stacie flushed with embarrassment.

"I guess I should have been more specific than 'late morning.' Or maybe I'm an alien from another time zone."

Stacie decided to relax; being caught vacuuming in her sweats was not the end of the world.

"It's only 10:00 A.M.," she said in mocked irritation and shook a finger at him. "That's mid-morning, not late morning."

"Shall I go away and come back in an hour?" he offered.

"Don't be ridiculous," Stacie said, reaching for his wrist and moving him toward a chair in the living room. "But you'll have to amuse yourself out here while I get changed. Maybe you can get the vacuuming done." She left him and cheerfully disappeared down the hall.

The opportunity for a long, hot shower was gone, but Stacie went into the bathroom to wash her face and brush her teeth. Then she went to her closet to select some fresh clothes. Suddenly, she burst out in laughter when the whirr of the vacuum cleaner filled the apartment. The moment of

embarrassment had completely passed, and she was beginning to be genuinely optimistic about the day for the first time.
If he could put her at ease so simply, it was bound to be an
enjoyable, relaxing day.

And she would not have to think about Brad. She could
revel in the marvelous weather, take snapshots of the animals,
and dream with Dillon about the new shelter. Brad had not
called in the four days since their last casual meeting. Somehow she had thought that the news about working in Weston
would have been enthusiastically received by Brad. His with-
drawal had shocked her, and every day that went by without a
phone call befuddled her more.

Dillon and Brad were so different and seemed to want
different things from her. Sometimes it was hard to figure out
what she wanted from herself. Yes, she needed to get away
from all of this.

She pulled on some gray cotton slacks that she would have
ironed if there were more time, put on a red shirt, and then
scrounged around in the closet for some comfortable walking
shoes. Her hair could hang loose, she decided after brushing it
thoroughly. Pulling a white sweater off a hanger, she was
ready to go.

It was a perfect day for the zoo. The sun was shining, but it
was not uncomfortably hot, and it was too early in the summer
for the bees to be as bothersome as they would be in a few
weeks. Stacie had not been to the zoo since she had come with
Megan's Sunday School class almost two years ago. Even
before they arrived, she cautioned Dillon that the zoo contained more than they could comfortably see in one day. As
soon as they were inside the gate, Dillon stopped to study the
map.

"What's your favorite animal?" he asked.

Stacie laughed. "I never really thought about it. Elephants, I guess."

"Then we go this way." Dillon pointed confidently to the left. "On the way there we can see the monkeys and the birdhouse. Oh, and the snakehouse."

Stacie grimaced. "I'll pass on the snakes, if you don't mind."

They strolled side by side along the blacktop path. Stacie's camera, hanging casually around her neck, gave her something to do with her hands when she started to feel nervous about being with Dillon. But it was not long before she relaxed completely and started really enjoying the day.

She stopped every now and then to snap a photograph and although she was taking pictures of the animals, she always managed to capture a child in the frame as well. As she had expected, the zoo was swarming with families. Some of the children were cranky and hungry—it was almost lunch time—but most of the ones Stacie noticed were fascinated by the animals, and she was delighted by watching them. Her zoom lens allowed her to capture their expressions without disturbing their natural reactions.

"I didn't know you were a photographer," Dillon said after she clicked a shot of twin girls surveying the African elephants.

Stacie shrugged. "It's just a hobby. I like photographing children."

Dillon raised an eyebrow. "Maybe we could get some of your shots blown up and hang them at the new shelter."

"I'm not sure they'll be good enough for that," she said hesitantly.

"You never know until you try."

"Some of the families that come to the shelter might be there awhile," Stacie said. "I'd like to organize an outing for the children. If we could find transportation, we could bring a group here."

Dillon nodded in agreement. "It would be a real treat." He scanned the menu of the concession stand they were approaching. "Are you hungry? It looks like they have your basic hot dog or your basic hot dog."

Stacie smiled. "What's a trip to the zoo without a hot dog?"

With their hands full of food, they found an empty bench and claimed it. They sat contentedly munching and watching the streams of people pass by. Intermittently, they chattered about the animals, zoos they had visited when they were children, plans for the Weston shelter, and favorite childhood pets. Dillon had Stacie nearly hysterical with laughter by recounting the antics of the puppy he got for his tenth birthday. Eventually, Dillon consulted the map again, and they resumed their leisurely tour of the zoo.

Stacie had to admit she was having a wonderful time. Just like the other times when she had been with Dillon, he had a knack for making her relax and enjoy herself, free of the weight of her personal problems. Purposely she had kept Dillon separated from the rest of her life. Other than knowing a little about the work she was doing at the camp, he did not know any of the people or experiences that were important to her. He did not know about Megan nor about how involved she was in her church; he certainly did not know about Brad. When Dillon and Stacie were together, it was almost as if those other things did not exist, and in those brief times, she found welcome respite.

But she knew this was not real. Sooner or later, the two worlds would have to meet.

Her feet ached at the end of the day. Unquestionably she was relaxed and had relished every moment of the day. Dillon put his arm around her shoulder as they walked up the sidewalk to her door, and for the first time all day she felt reality striking. She had willingly held his hand on and off all day, because she had a genuine affection for him, but she was unsure how to handle what was certain to come next.

She knew Dillon expected that she would invite him in. It was not even supper time yet, and they could easily spend the evening together as well. It was an awkward moment when they reached the door for she knew he was waiting for her to give some signal about whether the date would end or not.

Stacie pulled her keys out of her pocket and turned to Dillon. "I had a wonderful time," she said, and then laughed. "That sounds trite, I know, but I did have a nice day."

"Let's not wait so long before we do something together again," Dillon said. "Of course, after we're settled in Weston, it'll be a lot easier to see each other."

Stacie nodded but did not say anything.

Dillon seemed to understand that she was not going to ask him to come into the apartment. "Goodbye, Stacie," he said, and then he leaned down to kiss her.

She turned her face up to his like she had in the past, but pulled away after only a brief kiss.

"What's wrong?" Clearly, Dillon was puzzled.

"I'm sorry, Dillon."

"Sorry about what? Don't you feel well?"

"I've really enjoyed the time we've spent together," she said, looking down at her hands and twisting her keys between her fingers. "When I'm with you, it's so easy to relax and be myself."

"But?" he asked.

"But . . . I don't think it's a good idea for us to keep seeing each other—personally, I mean."

Dillon was bewildered. With a sigh, he leaned against the brick building and searched her face for some explanation. "This doesn't make any sense, Stacie. I thought we were both enjoying each other."

"We were!" She was quick to reassure him. "I like you a lot. But I just don't think. . . ."

"I get it," Dillon said with a flash of insight. "There's another man." It was a statement, not a question.

Given Brad's reaction at the hospital four days ago, Stacie was not sure how to answer Dillon. But at that moment, she realized that what Brad felt did not matter so much as what she felt. She enjoyed Dillon—there was no question about that. But she loved Brad.

fifteen

"There you go, Mrs. Haskins," Stacie handed the plate to the middle-aged woman with wispy brown hair. "Enjoy your lunch." She smiled mechanically, as she had for all the other people who had come through the lunch line that day. As soon as Mrs. Haskins turned her back, Stacie's smile disappeared.

Stacie automatically scooped up another serving of tuna casserole and stood poised to plop it on a plate. After a moment she realized no one was there to receive it. It was after 1:00 P.M., and the line had trickled down. She studied the tangled mess of noodles balanced on the oversized serving spoon; a pasty mixture held the strands together, the bland whiteness broken up only by an occasional bright green pea or a glimpse of tuna. Actually, it did not look too bad, as far as tuna casserole went. Now that the line was finished, Stacie could sit and eat if she wanted to. But she did not have much of an appetite.

Tired, Stacie sat down on the three-legged wooden stool behind her. Cheap, bent flatware clanked and scraped against plastic dishes as the crowd of about forty chased after every morsel of their daily hot meal. Two large coffee urns were nearly ignored; only the very faithful were drinking coffee in the June heat. Stacie picked up a wet rag and absently wiped a spot off the table where there was nothing to be wiped. If she could just keep busy, she told herself, she would not have time to feel sorry for herself.

Dillon had been in the office most of the morning, working at his little table in the reception area and using Marsha's phone. It was a good thing Stacie did not know beforehand that he was going to be there; she would have been unbearably nervous about going to work. As it was, she simply followed her usual routine and went to the office, where there was plenty to occupy her mind and hands.

Every time Dillon spoke to her, Stacie's heart raced. Her throat throbbed with a rapid pulse and her ears seemed to clog up. Dillon, on the other hand, remained calm and cool all morning. Cordial as always, he interacted freely about their project. Never once did he hint at what she had said Saturday or make any reference to their personal relationship. To her surprise, he seemed to accept easily his own insight that there was another man who had a hold on Stacie's heart. But, one morning of being in the same building would not tell the whole story. Stacie could not help wondering what it would be like to be with Dillon everyday. *Would she regret her decision not to get involved with him? If he gave her another chance, would she take it?*

Stacie had let Dillon believe that, yes, there was another man. But was there? Brad had let another weekend go by without phoning her, and once again he had not been in church. Normally, he hated to miss even one Sunday, so missing two Sundays in a row meant something was wrong. And Stacie felt responsible. She had willingly given up Dillon—and had no regrets—but apparently she did not have Brad, either.

Scanning the room, Stacie saw that most of the people were finished eating. The cart outside the kitchen door was accumulating a stack of dishes as people cleared their own tables. Most of them would spend the rest of the day outside in the fine weather; a few would linger around the shelter during the afternoon lull and eventually settle in for the night. With a few exceptions, Stacie would see them all again when she came back to help on Thursday. These were the people she had dedicated her life to; these were the people who needed something which she could give. Some of them had been eating and sleeping at the shelter for months and they were very familiar to her.

Still, she did not know them, and they did not know her. She knew their circumstances, and she worked hard to help them get back on their feet. If she did her job well, then they moved on and others drifted in to fill their places around the lunch tables. *Would her whole life be that way,* she wondered, *full of people who floated in when they needed her and moved on when they did not? Would there ever again be a man in her life who wanted something other than hot food and low-cost housing? Would she ever be close to someone who saw past the job that she did to the reason why she did it?*

Rising abruptly from the stool, Stacie shook off her musings and concentrated on the task of cleaning up. She wheeled the metal cart, laden with tottering plates and cups, into the kitchen.

The phone in her office rang for about the tenth time that day. Normally, Stacie did not mind interruptions, but at this rate, she would never get through the stack of work she had assigned herself for the day.

"Stacie Hanaken," she mumbled into the receiver.

"Hi, Stace."

Stacie dropped her pencil and sat up. "Hi, Brad." He had not said enough for her to judge his mood, but she cautiously asked, "How are you?"

"I'm fine."

"Busy, I suppose."

"Yes, there's plenty to do." Brad paused and got to the point. "Stacie, I just called to let you know they're finally going to let Mrs. Barrows out. I'm going to take her home this afternoon. Maybe you'd like to come along."

"Absolutely! What time?"

"Can you meet me at the hospital at 4:00 P.M.?"

Stacie looked at her watch, and then at the pile of work on her desk, and then back at her watch. "Four o'clock is fine."

"I'll see you then."

Brad hung up and left Stacie sitting in the chair listening to silence on her end of the phone. Slowly, she replaced the receiver in the cradle and sank back in her chair.

It was a few minutes after 5:00 P.M. when they arrived at the cottage. Brad maneuvered the van as close to the door as he possibly could. Mrs. Barrows sat sideways on a bench in the back with her legs, in casts, propped straight out in front of her. As soon as the engine was turned off, Stacie released her seatbelt and squeezed through the front seats to get to Margaret. Brad already had the wide door of the van open.

"I think I can just lift her out, Stacie," he said.

"Don't talk about me as if I weren't here," Mrs. Barrows chided. "I've got two broken legs, but my ears are fine."

"Yes, ma'am," Brad answered, putting his face close to hers with a grin. "May I help you out of the van?"

"Yes, you may. I'm hardly in a position to quibble about your offer, am I?"

"Stacie, I took the wheelchair out of the back. Why don't you make sure it's locked open, and I'll just lift her down into it."

Immediately Stacie hopped out of the van and stood behind the wheelchair. She positioned it close to the van door and carefully checked to be sure the chair's wheels were locked.

"Okay, Mrs. B.," Brad said, "on the count of three. One, two, three."

With a smoother motion than Stacie would have thought possible, Brad whisked Mrs. Barrows out of the van and into the wheelchair.

"Well, that was certainly a fine job, Bradley," Mrs. Barrows commended. "I didn't feel the least bit insecure."

"Now we'll get you in the house and make sure you have everything you need," Stacie said. When they arrived, she had noticed a small gray car parked across from the cottage, but she could not quite remember who it belonged to. Obviously, someone was there to care for Mrs. Barrows—but who?

She unlocked the wheels and started pushing. The front door of the cottage was only a few yards away, but the stone path was not conducive to a smooth wheelchair ride. Stacie could see Mrs. Barrows literally bobbing up and down with the bumps.

"Stacie, dear," Mrs. Barrows said mildly, "who issued you a driver's license for this contraption? Rather a rough ride, don't you think?"

Stacie laughed. "Sorry. I'll get better with practice, I'm sure."

The front door opened up just then, and Stacie saw who it was that had arrived in the gray car—Jenna McLean.

"Jenna, honey, how kind of you to be here so early," Mrs. Barrows said cheerfully. "I wasn't expecting you until later."

"I wanted to be here when you got home."

"I hope I haven't inconvenienced you too much. You're being very sweet to come stay with me for a few weeks."

So it was Jenna McLean who would be taking care of Mrs.

Barrows. It had not occurred to Stacie that Jenna could do this, but it made perfect sense. She was a college student with no classes during the summer weeks, and she was going to be a camp counselor on the weekends anyway.

"Hi, Stacie," Jenna said, putting her hands on the handles and pushing the chair into the middle of the living room. "How's our patient?"

"She has been quite cooperative," Stacie reported light-heartedly, "and I'm sure she will thrive in your capable hands."

"I'll do my best," Jenna said.

Stacie had been momentarily flustered when she realized that Jenna would be caring for Mrs. Barrows, but she quickly came around to appreciating the sacrifice Jenna was making of her summer vacation in order to do it. Jenna would do a good job. Despite her schoolgirlish approach to Brad, Jenna seemed sincere and obviously had genuine affection for Mrs. Barrows.

"Why don't I fix us all some tea," Stacie suggested.

"Be sure to put fresh water in the kettle," Mrs. Barrows instructed. "The teabags are on the shelf next to the sink. I'm sure there's no fresh cream after all this time away—"

"Mrs. Barrows, please relax," Stacie laughed. "I'm quite experienced at brewing tea, I assure you. I'm sure I can find everything I need."

Amused, Mrs. Barrows retreated. "Very well. Get on with it, then."

Stacie swung open the door to the kitchen and looked around. Jenna had come early enough to tidy up and make the kitchen sparkle. The copper teakettle gleamed on the back burner of the stove. Stacie lifted it and filled it with water. The old gas stove had to be lit with a match, but it took only a moment to find one. She leaned against the counter and watched to make sure the flame caught properly.

Satisfied with her success, she turned her attention to finding mugs and the blue and white porcelain teapot Mrs. Barrows always used when she served tea. Stacie thought it was a nice twist to be able to make tea for Mrs. Barrows, who always insisted on fussing over everyone who came into her home. Her injuries would force her to accept the attention she deserved from other people, and that was a thought which pleased Stacie.

With the swinging door shut, Stacie could hear only muffled voices from the other room interspersed with brief outbursts of laughter. No doubt Mrs. Barrows had found yet another story to tell to her captive audience, and they relished it. Although curious about the story, Stacie savored the moments alone in the kitchen. The ride from the hospital had been tense—both because she was concerned that Mrs. Barrows was not comfortable and because Brad spoke to her only in limited ways. She even wondered why he had bothered to invite her along. Now she heard him laughing freely with Jenna and Mrs. Barrows and became even more convinced that she was the cause of whatever was disturbing him.

The kettle whistled. Stacie quickly turned off the gas and poured the steaming liquid over the teabags in the porcelain pot. The familiar tray that Mrs. Barrows always used was nearby, and Stacie arranged the pot and four mugs on the tray, with sugar and lemon, and carried it into the other room.

"There don't seem to be any fresh pastries around," Stacie teased, "so we'll have to make do with just tea."

"I suppose it will be quite some time before I can do any baking," Margaret lamented.

"It's the perfect opportunity for me to learn," Jenna said

enthusiastically. "You can let me be your hands and feet for a while, and maybe I'll pick up a few tips."

Mrs. Barrows tilted her head toward Jenna. "I'm a very strict instructor, you know."

"And I'm a very quick learner," Jenna answered right back. "And we'll have lots of time together."

Stacie felt a pang of jealousy. It was silly, of course. It was impossible for her to leave her job all summer and spend it with Mrs. Barrows, as appealing as that sounded. The important thing was that Mrs. Barrows had someone to look after her, and Jenna was a perfect candidate.

"I'm afraid I have to spoil the party," Brad said, swallowing the last of his tea. "I have to get back to town." He turned to Jenna. "Do you have everything you need?"

Jenna nodded. "I stopped at the grocery store on my way here."

"Call if you need anything at all."

Again, Jenna nodded.

"Ready, Stacie?" Brad asked her, without really looking at her. Suddenly, she realized that was what she had found so strange about his behavior all afternoon. For as long as she had known Brad, he had always looked her directly in the eye, even when she tried to avoid his gaze. Now he seemed not to look at her at all. In fact, he seemed more interested in Jenna. *Or was it her imagination?*

"I'm ready when you are," Stacie said, awkwardly bumping the coffee table with her knee as she stood up.

The ride back to town was very quiet. From the start, it was evident that Brad was not in the mood for conversation—not with Stacie, anyway—and there was no point in pushing him. She knew him well enough to know that when he was ready to talk, he would. She only hoped it would be soon. For weeks she had treated him this way and he had every right to be cool towards her. But deep inside, she clung to the belief that his true feelings were much different, and eventually they would surface.

Brad brought the van to a slow stop along the sidewalk outside Stacie's apartment. He made no move to get out, but she had not supposed that he would.

With her hand on the door handle, Stacie said, "Thanks for including me in taking her home, Brad."

Brad shrugged and looked out the window. "We were together when we found her; it seemed logical to take her home together."

Logical. Stacie repeated the word in her mind. It was a word distinct from feeling, divorced from emotion. Logical. Brad had called her because it was the logical thing to do.

"Well, good night, Brad."

"Good night, Stacie."

Before driving off, Brad courteously waited until she reached her door and unlocked it. With the door half open, she stood under the dim porch light and watched him pull away.

Had he pulled away from her completely? Would the image of his new van disappearing into traffic linger in her mind? She had hoped for so much more.

sixteen

The morning was getting away from Stacie much too quickly. For weeks she had looked forward to opening day at the camp but now that it had come, she did not feel ready.

For one thing, the opening of the camp meant that soon she would start working in Weston, and she had done nothing about finding a new apartment. Several trips to the grocery store had yielded dozens of boxes suitable for packing. A few of them now contained some books and magazines or miscellaneous dishes wrapped in towels, but most of them lay in a flattened pile in the living room, daring Stacie to begin packing in earnest. If she had been moving to Thomasville, she would have been ready but Weston was close enough that she did not really have to move until she was sure she wanted to. Never had it occurred to her not to move nearer her new job—until it came time to pack. She was reluctant to read the apartment listings in the Weston newspaper. For the time being, she decided she would make the long drive back and forth.

Stacie haphazardly slapped butter on her toast and hastily crammed it into her mouth, chasing it with a swallow of orange juice. That was all the breakfast she had time for now and she knew there would be plenty to eat at the Homestead later this morning.

The phone rang, just as she forced the last lump of bread down her throat. "Hello," she said.

"Good morning!"

"Hi, Megan. Ready for the big day?"

Megan laughed skeptically. "Time will tell how prepared

we are." She paused to get to the real reason for her early morning call. "Stacie, I've got so much junk to take out there, I'm running out of space in the car. And I promised Donna I would give her a ride, her car's in the shop."

"Again?"

"Yep. I don't think there will be room for all three of us."

Stacie moaned. "So I have to drive out there by myself?"

"I'm sorry. We could caravan if you'd like."

"No, go ahead. I need a few more minutes to get ready, anyway." Stacie glanced at the clock. "I'll see you out there in about an hour." Disappointed, she hung up the phone. But she did not have time to wallow and she immediately moved on to the next task.

Four gallons of red fruit punch concentrate sat on her kitchen table. She would have to lug those out to her car, to begin with, and they were heavy enough that it would take two trips. Without further procrastination, she loaded up her arms and started out the door. She was nearly out when the phone rang. With her foot propping the door open and her arms full, she hesitated only a moment before deciding to let her answering machine pick up the call. Whoever it was would have to wait until she lightened her load a little.

Outside, she crinkled her face at the weather; it was not the bright, sunny day they had all hoped for. She would definitely have to take a sweater out to the camp for the opening ceremonies. The sky was gray and cloudy, but it was just possible that the rain would hold off long enough for them to enjoy their festivities. The ceremony would be brief, just Pastor Banning making an introduction and Mrs. Barrows welcoming the campers and their families. After that, the picnic would start and everyone would be free to roam the acreage as they pleased.

Stacie made one more trip to the car with the rest of the

punch concentrate and a sack of plastic silverware. As an afterthought, she put in the only lawn chair she owned and slammed the trunk closed.

By the time she got back inside, the light on the answering machine was blinking. She whizzed by the machine and snapped on the play button on her way to the closet for a sweater. She stopped in her tracks when she heard the voice on the phone.

"Hi, Stacie. Megan said you'll be driving down by yourself. I thought maybe you'd like to ride with me instead. Maybe you're already on your way, and that's why I got your machine, but just in case I'll stop by on my way out of town." Click. The message ended.

Stacie slowly retraced her steps to the phone in disbelief. *Why would Brad suddenly call on the morning of opening day, after days—almost weeks of an impenetrable silence? Had Megan put him up to this? Worse, had Megan contrived the whole thing? Had Donna's persistent car trouble become an excuse for throwing Stacie and Brad together?*

She looked at her watch. If she hurried, she could be ready to leave in ten minutes, and maybe she could be gone by the time Brad arrived. On the other hand, she was curious about why he suddenly called and sounded so pleasant. If she left now, she would never know the answer.

In shocked slow motion, Stacie went to the bedroom and picked up her hairbrush. She tugged it through her thick hair until both her hair and her emotions were under control, and then pulled her hair back and off her neck in a sleek, silky ponytail. Her crisp white shirt and blue walking shorts looked very sporty and camplike. When the doorbell rang, she knew she would answer it.

"Hi, Brad. Sorry I missed your call."

"That's okay. I saw your car and figured you were still

here." He smiled nervously. "I don't have anyone else riding with me. If you want to, maybe. . ."

Stacie had never known Brad to leave a sentence hanging in the air that way. She nodded awkwardly herself. "Sure. I've got some things . . . in my car. . . . That's where I was when you called. . . . I'll just get my keys." Self-consciously, she left him standing in the doorway while she fetched her keys from the kitchen counter.

When the trunk sprang open, Brad immediately reached in for the load. The early summer sun had already bronzed his face and arms, evidence of his hard work. Stacie involuntarily admired his muscles, bulging slightly, as he efficiently transferred the punch concentrate from her trunk to the back of his van. She followed meekly with the lone lawn chair—feeling silly with only one now that she was not alone.

In a few minutes, they were on their way. Brad sat comfortably in the driver's seat, and Stacie, on the passenger side, tried to keep from staring at him while she wondered what this was really all about.

The gray clouds lost their innocence and spat a mist at the earth below. "Wouldn't you know it," Brad said, "rain for opening day."

Stacie shrugged one shoulder. "It's not really raining. Maybe it will clear up before we get there."

"I hope so. I don't think everyone will fit in the dining hall." He flicked on the windshield wipers. "Maybe this will help a little."

"I haven't had a chance to tell you how nice the van is," Stacie said. "I'm glad it all worked out for you."

Brad smiled but kept his eyes on the road. "It sure makes my life a lot easier. And having the logo on the side is worth a hundred billboards." He started chuckling. "One guy said that

he called my company because he'd seen one of our vans—
made it sound like we had a whole fleet out there. I guess
because I get around to so many places, he thought there must
be more."

"Then things are still going well."

"Just great." Brad sounded genuinely enthusiastic. "The
guys I have working for me are doing a terrific job. Lon's wife
just had a baby, and he brings new pictures all the time. I keep
threatening to put an extra bolt in his neck to make sure his
head stays attached."

Stacie sat and listened to Brad ramble on about the projects
he was working on. Although she was interested in everything
he had to say, she could not help thinking that this was not the
reason he had come by to drive her to the Homestead. One
moment, she enjoyed their casual conversation; the next
moment, she desperately wanted him to get to the point. But
she said nothing of how she felt.

"Look!" Brad said, leaning over the steering wheel and
pointing forward. "Isn't that an incredible rainbow?"

Stacie leaned forward and immediately caught his enthusiasm. "I can see the complete arch—and it looks like it's
coming down right in the middle of the Homestead."

Brad looked directly at her, for the first time all morning,
and grinned. "Do you suppose Mrs. Barrows has a secret she
hasn't told us about?"

Stacie joined right in. "Something about little green people
with funny accents who keep the camp going?"

They watched, spellbound, as the road they followed
seemed to lead them straight to the end of the iridescent arch
of colors. By the time they reached the Homestead, the mist
had gone—and with it the rainbow.

The grounds of the camp were so crowded that there was hardly a suitable place to park the van. Nevertheless, Brad confidently backed into a tight space Stacie never would have attempted to put her car into, much less a full-size van. Somehow she scrounged up the determination not to squeeze her eyes shut as he maneuvered into the spot at the beginning of the circular road. As soon as they were out of the van, the crowd swallowed them up. Stacie turned to say something to Brad, but he was gone.

She scanned the lawn for him and spotted him, but he did not look back at her, and she knew she was on her own. Still befuddled about why he had offered her a ride, Stacie retrieved two gallons of punch concentrate from the back of the van and started toward the dining hall. She ducked to avoid being attacked by a soccerball in flight and gave it a swift kick as it rolled across her path. The scene before her was a whole new place—the kind of place Margaret Barrows had been describing to her all through the spring weeks. Children, parents, and counselors in distinctive tee shirts swarmed the central lawn. Megan was busy passing out photocopied maps showing the camp buildings and trails. Pastor Banning was putting the finishing touches on a makeshift platform for the opening ceremony. With the rain gone, the day could not be more perfect.

Jenna emerged from the cottage, capably steering Mrs. Barrows and her wheelchair across the lawn.

"Stacie, dear, isn't it a marvelous day?" Margaret's eyes were bright and nearly twinkling with pleasure.

"Absolutely perfect," Stacie answered, leaning over to kiss a pink cheek. "Everything looks great. Are you all set for your part?"

"Nothing will delight me more than officially reopening the Homestead."

"Here, Stacie," Jenna offered, "let me take that punch concentrate for you."

"Thanks, Jenna," Stacie said, grateful to be relieved of her load.

Mrs. Barrows gestured for Jenna's attention "You tell the girls in the kitchen that there's a big tub on top of the refrigerator that would be perfect for mixing the punch. And the wooden ladle with the long handle—"

"Please, Mrs. Barrows, relax!" Jenna rolled her eyes, then looked at Stacie. "She's been like this all morning. She refuses to believe that everything is under control."

Stacie clicked her tongue. "Whatever shall we do with her?"

"Oh, hush, both of you," Mrs. Barrows scolded.

"I'll be back in a few minutes." Jenna gripped a gallon in each hand and meandered toward the dining hall.

"In all the confusion this morning, I seem to have forgotten my watch." Margaret fidgeted in her chair. "What time is it, Stacie?"

"Just past 10:30 A.M. If Pastor Banning is ready, we should all be set to start at 11:00 A.M."

"I feel so useless, stuck in this silly chair," Margaret said, her frustration evident in her tone. "There's so much to be done."

Stacie put her hand on Margaret's shoulder and squeezed. "Everything is going according to plan. Just relax and enjoy the day."

"I thought you were coming with Megan," Mrs. Barrows said, abruptly changing the subject as she so often did.

"I was planning to, but I ended up riding with Brad."

"Oh?" Mrs. Barrows said hopefully.

"He called me this morning and offered me a ride."

"That's wonderful. It's always a pleasure to see the two of you together. Where is he now?"

Stacie shrugged. "I don't know. He's been acting strangely all day. As soon as we got here, he disappeared."

"Have the two of you sorted things out?"

Stacie lowered herself to the grass and crouched beside the chair. "I'm not sure. I can't figure Brad out today. I mean, he hasn't really talked about what was bothering him; but something is different, that's for sure."

"Perhaps I'll have a word with him today," Mrs. Barrows determined.

Amused, Stacie shook her head. "When he's ready to talk, he will."

Stacie believed what she said to Mrs. Barrows; she just hoped it would not be too long before Brad was himself again and gave some clue about what he was thinking. Stacie flinched as a badminton birdie whizzed by her left ear, keeping her from sinking into an ill-timed, reflective mood.

"Maybe we'd better check in with Pastor Banning," Stacie said, rising to her feet and releasing the brake of the wheelchair. She carefully maneuvered the chair across the lawn, trying to hit as few bumps as possible.

Outside the dining hall, a makeshift platform stood. It was constructed of odds and ends of lumber left over from the repair work Brad had done and was decorated by some of the children with bright crepe paper and balloons. Pastor Banning had insisted on including a short ramp off the left end so that Mrs. Barrows could be wheeled up to her rightful place.

"Good morning, Stacie," Pastor Banning greeted her enthusiastically.

"Everything looks terrific," Stacie said, gesturing widely. "Are you about ready to start?"

"I think so. Why don't you go ring the gong?"

"Gladly."

Stacie swung the mallet as hard as she could, several times in a row, and then watched, satisfied, as the attention of the crowd turned toward the platform. No doubt the campers would soon be scrambling over each other for the task of ringing the gong. Low, deep reverberations hung in the air as Stacie replaced the mallet on its hook.

It took only a few seconds to return to where she had left Mrs. Barrows—and she was surprised to see that Brad had taken her place behind the chair. Wordlessly, she stood next to him and looked up as Pastor Banning cleared his throat and started to talk.

"Greetings to all of you on this beautiful day that the Lord has given us," he said, sounding as if he were in the pulpit on a Sunday morning. "I am sure that each of you is enjoying your visit to the Homestead just as much as I am. It gives me great pleasure to present to you the woman who has made this camp possible for all of the children who are here today. Please welcome Margaret Barrows."

Pastor Banning started the applause which welcomed Margaret to the platform. With a broad smile on his face, Brad wheeled her up to a central point and returned to stand beside Stacie.

"When I closed down this camp several years ago," Mrs. Barrows began, "so that I could care properly for my husband, I did not know if I would live to see the day it was open again. I only wish David could be here beside me today. The Homestead was his dream to begin with; I was fortunate that he allowed me to share it with him." Her eyes filled with tears, and her voice had a faraway quality. "For fifty-three years I experienced the goodness of God through the love of David Barrows. He was steadfast in the lean times, a solace in sorrow, and always the spark of joy in my life. I wish you all could have known him."

Stacie's mind told her that Mrs. Barrows was talking to the whole crowd; her heart was hearing words meant just for her. She glanced up at Brad out of the corner of her eye—and felt the color rise in her face when she saw his gaze fixed on her. She turned back to listen to Margaret.

"I could tell you hundreds—thousands—of stories of this place in the years gone by. But the important thing is that you are here today, and hundreds of new stories will be told after you have gone because you were here. Welcome to the Old Family Homestead."

Stacie vigorously joined the zealous applause which followed Margaret's speech. In the midst of the crowd's response, she felt a touch on her shoulder. She turned her head slightly, and Brad grabbed both her hands before she could speak.

"I'm no David Barrows," he said, "and I don't know if I'll ever deserve to have anyone say those things about me. But if it happens, I want you to be the one, Stacie."

"Brad, I—"

"No excuses this time, Stacie, for either one of us. Let's get married."

Stacie gently pulled one hand away from Brad and fingered a gold chain around her neck. In a moment it was clear what was hanging from the chain: the simple diamond in a plain gold setting sparkled in the sunlight. She held it up for him to see, and he wrapped his hand around hers.

"I see you two have finally patched things up," said a cracking voice from the platform. "Bradley, you put that ring right back where it belongs."

"With pleasure!" Brad said, slipping the ring off the chain and onto Stacie's finger.

A Letter To Our Readers

Dear Reader:

In order that we might better contribute to your reading enjoyment, we would appreciate your taking a few minutes to respond to the following questions and return to:

Karen Carroll, Editor
Heartsong Presents
P.O. Box 719
Uhrichsville, Ohio 44683

1. Did you enjoy reading *A Matter of Choice*?
   ❑ Very much. I would like to see more books by this author!
   ❑ Moderately
   ❑ I would have enjoyed it more if

   _____

2. Where did you purchase this book?_____

   _____

3. What influenced your decision to purchase this book?
   ❑ Cover　　　❑ Back cover copy
   ❑ Title　　　❑ Friends
   ❑ Publicity　　❑ Other _____

4. Please rate the following elements from 1 (poor) to 10 (superior).
   ❑ Heroine   ❑ Plot
   ❑ Hero   ❑ Inspirational theme
   ❑ Setting   ❑ Secondary characters

5. What settings would you like to see in Heartsong Presents Books?

_____

_____

6. What are some inspirational themes you would like to see treated in future books?

_____

_____

7. Would you be interested in reading other Heartsong Presents Books?
   ❑ Very interested
   ❑ Moderately interested
   ❑ Not interested

8. Please indicate your age range:
   ❑ Under 18   ❑ 25-34   ❑ 46-55
   ❑ 18-24   ❑ 35-45   ❑ Over 55

Name _____

Occupation _____

Address _____

City _____ State _____ Zip _____

HEARTS♥NG PRESENTS books are inspirational romances in contemporary and historical settings, designed to give you an enjoyable, spirit-lifting reading experience.

LOVE A GREAT LOVE STORY?

Introducing Heartsong Presents —
Your Inspirational Book Club

Heartsong Presents Christian romance reader's service will provide you with four never before published romance titles each month! In fact, your books will be mailed to you at the same time advance copies are sent to book reviewers. You'll preview each of these new and unabridged books before they are released to the general public.

These books are filled with the kind of stories you have been longing for—stories of courtship, chivalry, honor, and virtue. Strong characters and riveting plot lines will make you want to read on and on. Romance is not dead, and each of these romantic tales will remind you that Christian faith is still the vital ingredient in an intimate relationship filled with true love and honest devotion.

Sign up today to receive your first set. Send no money now. We'll bill you only $9.97 post-paid with your shipment. Then every month you'll automatically receive the latest four "hot off the press" titles for the same low post-paid price of $9.97. That's a savings of 50% off the $4.95 cover price. When you consider the exaggerated shipping charges of other book clubs, your savings are even greater!

THERE IS NO RISK—you may cancel at any time without obligation. And if you aren't completely satisfied with any selection, return it for an immediate refund.

TO JOIN, just complete the coupon below, mail it today, and get ready for hours of wholesome entertainment every month.

Now you can curl up, relax, and enjoy some great reading full of the warmhearted spirit of romance.